The Wall In The Jungle

Journey Past Finding Your Safe Place

S D RODRIGUEZ

ADEODATUSTRAVELLINK

THE WALL IN THE JUNGLE

ISBN 979-8-218-17202-2

Library of Congress Control Number: 2024908108
February 2, 2024
United States Copy Right Office 1870

Published by

ADEODATUSTRAVELLINK
Bethesda, MD

Printed in the United States of America

10 9 8 7 6 5 4

<   >

Front & Back Covers Photo by Author

For David and Karen,

and Mom.

*For my sisters and to my brother, who's
ventures go far past our simpler times,*

*and to the youngest,
for whom we all must wait.*

And brats.

Contents

e

Acknowledgments:

Cream Album; the Man Song

Images:

Prologue, XIV, Tugboat, unknown, collection archive

Chapter 1, A 1972 Moto-Guzzi Eldorado 850, Harley-Davidson Saddle Bag, fiberglass faring, plexi-glass Shield, chromed Kit covers, Direct Drive 5-speed Trans & Overhead Cam engine

Chapter 7, A 1966 Chevrolet Nova 327 bored 0.30 over, milled 202 heads, Headman long-tube headers, Cherry-Bomb Glass-pack dual exhaust, ladder traction bars, G60/14" Sprint GT on Key-stone classics, Muncie 4-speed, short throw Hurst shifter, Thrush air shocks.

Chapter 25, Dunkin, Texron pre-60's, archive collection,

Chapter 59, Tru Williams, age unknown, pre-1970 Italy, archive collection

Chapter 60, Sailor, 1977, archive collection

Author

S D Rodriguez was born in Crystal City, Texas in 1957 to a struggling attorney and young spouse amid political unrest and cultural upheaval at the very beginnings of La Raza Unida and the after-math of WWII and depression of the Korean War, and starting of the Vietnam conflict. Unabashed racial discrimination was rampant, and he followed along to many relocations and experienced lifetimes changes hidden in the pages of military lifestyles. Luck, fate and experiences in our world found him in his first job at age 14 sacking groceries for tips at the Army Commissary on the Kreutzburg Kaserne in Zweibrucken, Germany.

Mr. Rodriguez served in the military onboard the aircraft carrier USS Dwight D. Eisenhower CVN-69, VA-65 Attack Squadron and TAD VQ-2 Reconnaissance Squadron at Rota, Spain. Retirement to the Security Industry led to a 20-year career in Washington, D.C., followed with an eventful four years of travel throughout the Upper-48 States and Canada. Later in life, he transitioned into private guarded transport with the assortment of U.S. Federal Agencies including the U.S. State Department, the U.S. Park Service, the U.S. Capital Police, the U.S. Library of Congress, the Washington District of Columbia Government, the U.S. Secret Service and High-Level Diplomatic Embassy concerns and as directed by the United States Government, including September 17, 2015 visitation of King Felipe VI (G'95) and Queen Letizia of Spain four-day visit to the U.S. to open the Joint Meeting of Spanish Scientists in the United State and Washington, D.C. and George Washington's Mount Vernon home in Virginia.

Prologue

Enter a dusty pre-2000 existence, ken to worlds anew, find solitude's meanings exposed by the tribute of fate.

Race wild in America's vastness where only hunters survive and the reality of yesterday was a mere necessity to survival.

Hope fades of any great acceptance in moving to new locations, finding just prejudice and discrimination. See our early American culture through a mysterious upbringing at a time of radical, social and cultural norm changes. Pack everything and venture anew to family-time trials held before the race to establish leaders intertwined in the new young wave shaped by events from around the world. A cultural means affected by political upheaval and wars.

Follow exciting experiences into a lifetime hidden in the archived pages of a military lifestyle.

An unconventional aspect of cultural identity.

THE WALL IN THE JUNGLE

Chapter 1

Wednesday 8 Sept. 1976

The pen falls upon a blank sheet of soft paper and from the assistance of some other muscle movement, words are spewed or thrown out on paper for all the world to see. It's difficult to imagine how it all comes to be, but it's here. It's the words, the thoughts, the movement – both negative and positive. The reach of tendons limited Pierce's imagination.

There is something about my bike, the front tire is not right on the rim tight as it shifts from side to side while the wheel turns. Someone said to flatten it and allow it to reset. I think the tire is messed up. Maybe I'll get a new one for the front and put the front one on the back and put the one on the back in the garage. That's what I'll do when I get the money to do it. But what if it's the rim that's bent?

Never mind.

She is mentioned in this journal well maybe because she fills my thoughts, or maybe just the thinking parts of my mind.

Montag, 13 Sept. 1976

Betsy was not a motorcycle. I suppose the comment made may still apply.

I slept last night, oh what, a daydream? I'd thoughts everything was all right, happy on the land of ours. It was raining mean as could be but a car kept swaying back to a gravel side of road. Water rushed in the drain ditch; trees whole trees swept away. Then there was a car in the ditch, just sitting there. The lady driving was scared, looking rattish and confused. She could not know why her car wouldn't start in the rain and all. So, we jumped into the ditch – it must've been about 20 feet wide and popped the hood. He believed it was a Camaro. Then from nowhere a dude in cut-offs jumped into the ditch kind of like diving into a pool. He must have hit the Mack truck because he didn't move for a bit.

The blue, the truck, completely submerged.

Over the front and simply smashed up to his head, no blood. That's when I woke.

The thing was my head was hurting – like from a hangover or something. But I didn't go drinking or anything the night before.

That was it.

17 Sept 1976

Imagine yourself, cruising, say 75 or 80 miles an hour, down some long and lonesome highway, winds blowing but because you're moving it is equivalent to that wind blowing, swatting hair from side to side. Looking below he sees only a swish of moving pavement. Topping the hill, a pair of red lights along the side of the road and immediately he begins down shifting, the engine screaming as it pops in from a lower rpm in a smooth split mini-second. One may only dream that black and white was not using radar. Sliding by the trooper sort of shakes his head, probably unknowingly relating when he was younger and more eager to experiment with some branded new toy.

Moto-Guzzi

He slowly breathes a sigh, as the rear view shows two orange parking lights along the side and no moving. More than certain he'd pinned 75 so God knows if that trooper was sleeping or maybe he wasn't even ever there. So, did you ever have one of those times when looking back to what happened, you're not sure?

18 Sept 1976

From here to there, eventually.

Quite a task it is.

What does he do if the thoughts just don't flow – don't even think?

Have you ever tried to dry your hair with a reading lamp? I'll tell you how it comes out.

Fleetwood Mac – tongues get tied every time they speak.

I'd like Fleetwood but not all his songs, just some.

Excuse me, he had to move the lamp to the other side.

Back now.

Van Morrison is also good. Leon Russel is good too.

So is Mary.

I could listen to Leon and Mary all day long. He wasn't drunk when he wrote this, but just half asleep.

I told you.

I'd make it.

Sept. 23, 1976

Went home Saturday. Dogs getting big.

Missy had pups.

About 4 weeks old.

Dalmatian.

Major is the father.

Parents are kind of strange, but they are cool.

Sometimes.

Broke my windshield on the way down. Stopped to put saddle-bag back together, bike just fell over onto guardrail. Plexiglass just crushed under extreme weight of bike. Came back Saturday night, minus a windshield. Bugs everywhere, glasses, eyes, teeth, hair.

Oh great, anyway I did have a great weekend. Saw a bunch of friends.

Jeff traded his Corvette for a Cougar. Ron and Petra are back together a lot, good football game on the weekend.

It seems as though these short writings keep getting shorter and shorter.

That would be great.

Sept 30,1976

It's hard to say, I guess I should say I wish the experience could be yours also.

Imagine this – Everything you might have wanted from home is now here. Relaxation sets in. Outside a train's horn blares in the night. The warm bed the cold night, the real music all contributes to some peaceful state which settle within the mind.

Finally, the transition from college seems to have faded into a new awareness of people, (Steven Stills is playing now) childish ways are happy memories. The pulling of hair, and kicking shins, deep inside.

Remember Lola Cherry Cola. Not having to be home at 12. Stranger even to not have to hide cigarettes from them, oh brother. All the lessons taught, making your bed, staying neat, respect and other thoughts as well, and they still have some meaning.

He looked gob smacked as she looked back at him. "The cake is stale, the thought, kind." she said.

"Fresh!" he heard her say as she turned and walked off.

Maybe some prudence would be shed for my problem. How am I going to submit 100 girl signatures? And numbers? And relationships?

Ronstadt sings some mean songs. Until next week then.

October 4, 1976

Yet another day goes by, where will it all end? I live my life as if to expect something tomorrow which I know is not right. A change must take place. The question is why?

Make no assumptions by reasons why, but marvel these possibilities. Look at the people - we all basically same, but notice how different everyone is, this is surely not by chance.

Oct. 16, 1976

Terror struck me, deep fear.

Another what?

The descriptions are the same.

They're usually full of rage, not a kind word.

"They'll kill you, save you, or even make you a god."

Now, some days they're frequency is more often than not. From out of nowhere they strike killing a few and wounding others.

As if the earth were turning over in bed, so does this terror affect us. Nowhere to hide, nowhere to go, no recognizable faces. Lost in a lost world.

Oct 27, 1976

A light blue car glides down that pavement with the greatest of ease, taking turn after turn as if the road were an arrow. The people within understand what is happening, but don't realize that man has really gotten this far. After cruising hour upon hour, the man says to his wife, "Let's stop at Donald's."

She says, "Okay."

The car turns into the restaurant and they kids fly into the sandy-smell filled place, each taking a different side to look for Ronald. Up to the counter the tykes run, stretching to make their chin rise above the cold aluminum counter. Bulging eyes roll from side to side, in search of that jolly clown with the big yellow shoes.

Into the restroom they both run, looking still for Ronald.

Finally, after giving up their search, they resort to violence. The lavatories of each bathroom are literally torn from the wall, the doors torn from their hinges. Tables are ripped from the floor and flung out through windows. The stainless-steel counter is smashed by blows of a force unknown to man. The lady frying the French fries is dunked time after time in the bubbling grease. The guy flip-ping the meat is shoved up through the exhaust fan getting sliced into large hunks of dead flesh. The little girl taking orders is thrown through the front doors and kicked about in the front yard. Walls are smashed, light fixtures torn away from the ceiling, the parking lot ripped up and moved with cars still upon it. Finally, the children give up, they can't find Ronald.

Suzie, the little girl, asks if they might go to Jack-In-The-Box, to see Jack.

Nov. 12, 1976

A short, short story.

It had been a nice quiet day until Johnny Boy came home. Johnny was a tall lanky guy burnt by the hot sun out west. His father had been a cowboy from the beginning, where he helped his father make saddle and break horses. Johnny's father died a couple years ago leaving only a small fortune for his mother. The little house was well furnished, and the yard well kept. One might expect to see a house like it in Home & Garden, but because its nowhere, no one really cared.

Johnny remembered the quiet days, when he and his father would go hunting or fishing, when his dad would make a special effort to be home on weekends and always bring the right things. Johnny slowly took the shotgun from the gun rack that afternoon, loaded it and commenced firing. Johnny was the last to see his screaming mother and Brandy the dog alive. He took his life as lonely people do with a long ear-piercing scream and a booming gunshot.

Nov. 27, 1976

The Last Entry: It was a dark and cold Monday morning, the night filled with tossing and turning. Bentley notified me of our position and situation, hinting something was in the air. I took it calmly as I always had.

"Captain!" Bentley blurted out.

"What is it Bentley, and make it quick, I've got a million things on my mind." I didn't really have a million things on my mind but felt like saying it, and Bentley was dense anyway.

"Captain, we're not where we're supposed to be, we should be in quadrant nine. We're in quadrant four. What should I do?" Bentley wasn't the brightest first mate to have, but he did follow orders.

"Get ahold of the Supreme Commander and tell him our position. If he cannot help us, no one can."

Back came Bentley with an ear shattering, "Yes Sir."

I watched as he stumbled down the long corridor and into the radio room. Something looked strange. In my position at the controls, I could plainly see everyone working. Snort the gentle giant easily raised a heavy piece as Morker the elf guided it and him past the small corner space aft. Portov, with his large hands kept everything polished and clean. Davip ran from one end of the room to the other, relaying numbers and words to Slur the Gluidior. The stearer Deco looked up at me with the simple question, "Where are we going?" I answered with a simple nod, assuring him I was in command. I knew where we were and Deco was a good man, he turned and proceeded on course.

"Bentley, where have you been?" I hit him hard with questions. He looked surprised.

"Captain, I was getting a bit to eat." Bentley squirmed his way out of this one, but he knew I'd catch up on him next time.

"Bentley, next time you get permission, or you'll burst yourself. Stand fast Bentley."

"Yes Sir!" he said shaking in his boots, I just had to be hard with him.

The next thing I knew, I was lying on the ground next to my commander chair. Bentley was helping me up and reporting damages, we had been hit. Repairs proceeded at UniNitrix-progress. Polnar scanned. Done. In my surprise, an old friend, teacher and co-captain at school was hovering some sixty klikes dead ahead.

...crack, "How ya' doing there Molic?" I radioed him.

"Just fine I be, at I'd surprised you with a little shot," he radios back.

..schachk, "Thanks, needed it, that. 'ere been?" he shouted.

...shhhc, "Up in four . . . uh," . . . ssshc, "a farther quadrant, back for a short. How'd things be back home?"

"ey're great. Molli sure be glad see yeh!"

I signaled to Bentley to go about with work. "What went on back out in quadrant thirteen?"

"Crack, oh, ohh nothing, just a small revolution."

"Crack", "Ooh really, well take care of this revolution you son of a gicsh!"

And with that I fired all I had at his racer. Bentley turned, his big question marked face staring at the pulsar explosion on Polnar's screen.

"Bentley, no one gets away with that. Let's get the devil out of here."

31 January 1977

. . . something in English today. I don't remember though.

"Write this down and 25 years from now you'll reread it and say I thought the same way 25 years ago."

8 February 1977

Somehow, every time he entered Ed's room, he'd lost way.

But that's not why I want to write in this book.

Dr Thompson figures it pretty good, but the number of grains of sand he counts isn't always the same.

Books, guns & time. What fun it is to sit and think a bit?

23 May 1977

Today is gonna be a great day!

Finally, I've found something that scares me but at the same time makes me happy.

Pennzoil Rig #101 Cactus is where I'll be spending the next three months & 20 days, 80 or 90 mile out into the Gulf of Mexico!

Flying in a helicopter at 80!

Making money! Today is gonna be a great day.

I can't even sleep. Time 12:40 AM and I'm wide awake.

June

Sunday.

Well things didn't turn out the way I thought that they would. I have one day left here and back to S.A. I go. This job is really poor. I'm cleaning up after a bunch of ignorant people. It irritates me. Even at $200 a week, I feel as though I'm wasting my time. There are few benefits though. Free meals, a bunk to sleep, not much work really, but I want more. I'm gonna have to check out San Antone` when I get back, even though I don't have a car.

Pause, think.

Chapter 2

Predawn, Pierce sat up as someone knocked at the base on the thick wooden door.

"I had shoes somewhere around here, I had them on when I left."

That was all he'd said as we took him to the back of the ranger sled. It sat low and we could see over top of the drifts without losing cover. Someplace down range from the bunker, they'd just emptied a full magazine into four trees only feet from zero. All fifteen slugs had left a mark, but only one had bull's-eyed the outlined head.

"It was I who's getting too old though and it seemed more so as I felt my karma slipping back to every other time."

He wanted to concentrate on work, I was swept back to a recent mission, or a time when something odd had happened.

Some times, their bodies we hadn't touched. Some places wrecked trucks we hadn't cleared. There were many places things had been left because we just couldn't go back to check to be sure. Once, we'd abandoned a troop carrier right in the middle of a cathedral church not long after the religious services ended, knowing no one could drive it and we'd never return to retrieve it. Even so, every now and again thoughts held me in trance.

He couldn't talk, I couldn't move.

Chapter 3

When Pierce was kidnapped and captured, we all knew he wouldn't be seen alive again. The individuals behind muzzled hand guns and black jump suits were underworld criminals. Whoever they were, they'd hit at 4 AM as all the world rested. In black-of-night, a heavy SUV skimmed along without notice, betting those Great Danes lay fast asleep.

As they turned up the drive, all the lights from the street fell dark, snaps and clips were the only sounds heard and as quickly as they'd arrived, they disappeared with their bound and blindfolded prey. Not a word had been spoken, no furniture knocked aside, and no clue was ever found.

Elizabeth Hawzeremi would be the last contact who he would talk with and when she made her mind up to complete the only covert mission commissioned to free him, we weren't surprised.

Just below the window sill by the big sofa sat his cat. He was big and had clawed his way up from under a table and sat across from Pierce.

"Wherever you been big fella?"

The big cat looked up at Dean who had been sitting staring at the window and then back to the window. Pierce felt quiet as he'd wronged Dean, stealing her away. He felt the drips on his sweaty back and sensed the hair on his neck raise. Almost instinctively animal like, he dropped off the chair and stood to face Pierce.

Caught off balance on slippery floor, Pierce fell up against the wall. "Don't do it Dean, I loved her too."

"You...every time I think of her, your stupid face comes to mind. I could put you away right here...now I mean..."

"Don't... think of what she would do, how would she support herself? I'm her only hope now."

"You're no help, look at her, she's lonely, anyway you're always gone."

"Right, you win," Pierce said looking off to his left, "take her then, I'll leave her."

Moving towards centre of the big kitchen, Dean pulled a pack out of his pocket and tapped out another cigarette. A crooked squashed white tube appeared as he clenched it between his teeth.

"I can't do that Pierce. She's always been free, that's how she wanted it. You never knew her very well, did you?"

He lit the crooked cigarette and sucked in a puff. Pierce moved up the wall a little as tiny drips of sweat appeared from his forehead.

"I don't think shooting me will solve anything, put the gun away."

"No, you moron, you're getting what you deserve. She had it all planned. Why do you think she left to Europe? How long ago did you last talk?"

"Then why a gun, and breaking in here, what do you want?"

"Shut up, sit back down, don't get up unless I tell you."

Moving to the phone, Dean reached over and picked up the receiver. With his left hand he punched in the numbers to a banker in Switzerland.

"What do you want? I'll make it all right for you, just tell me."

"Shut up, its too late now outlaw." He drew back on his cigarette and pointed at the door. "

"Get up and get in there. Slowly! Don't try anything stupid or you're another dead man."

"Okay, just don't shoot."

"She's gonna to want you to give her some numbers. You give her them numbers and we're good."

He pushed the lumpy prey through the door and over to a desk. "Open it."

"The safe?" He looked up and pushed the bottom of a book as a section of glued-together fake ones slipped out, then move sideways. A sparkly, twinkling dial gleamed back up at him.

"There's no money, the banks won't be open for another six hours. You'll get nothing."

"Hello Ma moitie`. . . yes, now okay?"

He handed the phone to Pierce. "Here, talk."

"Hello...no, but he has a gun, kill me he's said, no, sorry, no, I was never going to hurt you. What do you mean, from me?"

"Give her the numbers from accounts," he shouted, "and tell them bankers we're still married, and then say good-bye."

"I can't do that, you'd ruin me. My bank accounts are here, all my Swiss accounts. I'd go to jail."

"Would you instead like to be dead. Do it!"

Pushing him with the end of the gun. "It's that time Pierce, you got no choice. Read them numbers."

He smirked, and watched Pierce flip off a page, and begin "8-37-49223-34, yes 8-37-57422-28, uh-huh, yes, good. No, okay, just . . ."

"'Yes, bye." Dean said grabbing the phone.

He looked up at him and passed it back. "She'll be back later this evening."

"Okay, hello? Okay, you have what you wanted, now just leave me alone."

"Don't worry, get lost."

Facing the safe Pierce closed the book and placed it on the table. "You thief, you lousy thief. You'll never get away with all of this. Someday they will catch up with you, someday you'll have to pay it all back."

"Shut up and move over." Dean pulled the hammer back on the long barreled gun and aimed it at the bookcase to the right of where Pierce was standing. "Hurry pig."

"Well..." he faintly heard from the phone.

"Please don't' shoot. I'll keep quiet. I won't say anything to anybody, even the cops, okay? I won't go try to look, promise you man."

"Well, that's not how we planned it. Your keep quiet and live, you talk and somebody dies. Now shut up and sit down. Tape your ankles with this duct tape to the chair, don't know anything?"

"What do you mean. I gave her everything, she spent every dollar I gave her and still came back for more. The girl was on who knows what when she wrecked her Trans-Am. I couldn't do anything with her."

"You stupid idiot, didn't you see you couldn't love her. She used you, because she couldn't have what she really needed."

Dean motioned to Pierce to toss him the tape.

"Yeah, so she slept around, so what, you slept with her and didn't complain."

"Yeah, I slept with her. She knew, but I didn't hurt her, you hurt her. When she left, she was alone. She had nobody, she was confused and I was helping."

"Is that what you call help? You bastard. Treated her like a run-away. She became your toy, she lost her respect."

"So that's why huh, fell into her too. You'll never see her again," he said, "she's rich, I'm broke and you walk, it that it man?"

He looked down at Pierce and brushed back a wiry black strand of hair.

"That's right, that's all she has left and you took away any decency. I'm sorry Pierce." he said, and he pulled back the trigger.

Then again, later we stood in disbelief only to find out why she'd been killed too. The one person we all knew about, an assassin we'd feared but actually never seen put closure to her life.

Liz was good, but she also knew she was the only agent even capable of bringing P back from the nether world.

And we'd all given her the thumb-up go, along with some directional incentive to move quickly, finish ahead. One of our best, in her we never doubted she'd make it.

Throughout his mysterious years with the bureau, Pierce kept secrets no one else would ever have been able to sell. No person would stop to be any named part to a counter resistance within their struggle for justice and freedom. The Cuban guerrilla Felix Rodriguez worked closely with his American counterpart well into the 60's and just as the French Connection collapsed, Pierce's department had been able to forget about the rules, and place $14.57 million in convertible Swiss bank bonds. We never asked how he supported seven families, and well into 2000 there weren't ever any type of divestments nor investigative follow through. The bureau asked me once if I knew anything more, but no, I didn't.

Near Arlington, we'd agreed to meet at the McLean Family Restaurant for breakfast. It was an old meeting place, I'd been there with other under-covers, foreign agents and people working as informants. Pieces. Everyone knew we'd meet there, all the locals knew, but no one talked. Nothing.

Philip, the manager at the place knew us from the others and waved to the back area closest to a hidden exit. With an open alley way and quiet neighborhoods, and the back lot stocked with mission cars, we often staged for picks behind that little strip mall.

"Hey Menke!" he'd say in mid-eastern broken English.

My name wasn't Menke but I would watch him waving for me, and start moving past the table up front, a warm area by the windows. A couple bunches of coats hung on eye level coat-racks with the smells of hot pancakes and buttery syrup.

"Hey Philippe`, some business today, okay?"

"OK Mr. Menke, always busy, but they have table for you, is good."

They'd make a way through the mismatched tables, around past the long counter across the griller near to four square tables. Before we asked, cups were filled and chilled water set out.

"Thanks Philip, you always know…"

"It's no problem for me, but I know you for many years and we have some new boys, so water is Okay?

"Well let's keep it that way, uhm, um, say breakfast, over-easy, bacon, some rye-toast, and give TB the same. He's cutting back on carbs, hash brown off his plate, no hash brown potato."

"Okay, take away, you see tomato juice this morning?"

Chapter 4

Ri met us inside just as we'd finished. He was seldom late, so they asked if anything, what was going on, what we should know about. He swore not to worry. Nothing anyone would believe anyway. Shrugging off, he dropped down to the business briefing.

Presumably, they had taken a foreign contact, we were to pick up and deliver in Justice. Seemed simple enough, drive over into Washington on a beautiful spring day. Pierce pulled up just as we were leaving and followed us down towards National. At any time on any day, the mystery of a long backed-up line of traffic faded with the lifting fog, or but a deer pulled down off to the roadside, past Windy Run and the sprinkle of tourists out walking the over-looks searching for some memorial. Washington Parkway traffic floated down under Key Bridge, then along side Roosevelt Island and past some joggers jogging.

We slipped a lane over then coasted along side some bean-counter moving off on another first exit. We stayed, straight true and sped under the ridge passing charcoal concrete archways, then out past another exit and down under overgrown bunches of trees. They went along, passing the northwest reaches of Arlington Cemetery, added some quick brake tap stops, then as those speed-demons Pentagon employees exited, we bullied on, flying through another underpass searching some great views of Washington. Star rays glistens out toward them. The largest buildings reached up to look across to island trees. Their reflections came across the river, and we'd watched them curve down and out into new day sun, past the shadows slow gaze crawling. Two lines of cars melded into a single row of taxis.

Midnight Washington DC

To our right, Columbia Island Marina, our boats tied and covered-over from morning mist rain. Tall trees waved off the breezes and seemed to be hiding in the dusted ground. Reminiscent of the prisoner's gates into the Tower of London where the steps were seldom dry. We'd worked from docks once, running informants back through that secreted portal, an underwater tunnel to the Pentagon barely even noticeable with low tide. About enough slip to grasp tight boot straps. Our blacked-out boat, overpowered and under-kept, we stay up with the quickest Homeland response skiffs. Every one of those jobs was immediately turned over to CIA, no questions, no second guesses.

Over a hump-back bridge, they slowed down to allow traffic moving in and away from the lanes pointing south. Around a long sweeping right turn, they coasted into the airport as all the yellow DC cabs and metro-locals did. The more uncertain drivers always slowed down, to clog the then obviously unbelievable free-for-all of traffic moving toward the old airport buildings, the original airport.

"When's he due in?"

Chapter 5

"G-27, clearing north, client is leaving restaurant, route B, ETA at 20 minutes."

"Have a nice drive '27, base clear."

"Base, all units cover B route, clearing court, '27, 2 minutes down range at this time out."

Echo Smith blaring out from the in-dash CD, "...wish that I could be like the cool kids, like the cool kids...".

Richards had led that day. As we arrived, his wagon clipped the curb, maybe a piece of glass. We watched as he jumped back, looking around checking the rear tires. As fast as he'd scrambled out, the wheel flattened.

Pierce chuckled a bit as they watched the forty-two year vet kneel down and cry. The man-person cowering, playing out the kid who'd dropped his ice cream cone, almost weak from frustration. We watched him pull the jacket open and reach with his other hand.

"Oh no!" they thought. Time slowed to an unbelievable stop as his arm fell from inside his jacket and extended.

"Base, yeah uh G22, fix-a-flat to current location, out of service and transport down, scratch destinations, we are delayed."

Base was quiet. "two-two, you know that's on you, third time."

"Copy base, copy, turn around eta?"

A longer silence, we were thinking they were taking bets.

"Base G22, relieved 4 hours, stand down, we are sending backup to your location, clear this channel."

Richards looked at me, shrugging just enough.

"Rich, see if you can get any closer, you're in two lanes."

"What?"

"Back up man, get it back on your side."

Across the street an airport demo-crew was working with their little yellow dinosaur-nosed tractor scooping deep in mud, one workman propped up by his shovel. Ground rumbles and screeches from the scraping claw and we only shuddered halfway drawing side pieces at the noise. It seemed to angled in as if a hunter begging for reptiles to come wiggling out, anticipations building quickly. Another time, almost but just another "clunk, clunk". About ten feet back, a white and green tool truck stood parked, its motor bleeding black smoke, the orange strobe pop-up-cones spaced here and there to slow cars down along .

None of cars slowed.

We cleared right, then back behind, then the mezzanine. Looked right, felt right, we were moving him in. Both rear doors open, the two passengers searched the blinding light for "someone", oddly or not, in their own words. As we expected, no one from the inside moved from their post and we entered the building, our hands stuck to weapons.

"Colonel, your subject jumped Red Dragon, we'll hold our positions at 20th and C".

It was then that our passenger turned to us clutching and raising the brief case.

"You guys do good job, watch your heads."

"Got it, okay, let's move, we're on station in fifteen."

"Hey, you guys," our passenger yelled back in his broken English. He had propped the case on the scanner table, squeezing it turned it around and opened it. Enough buy a battalion, you know that, tanks, life pretty good to this. So bad you play everything top line, you Americans."

We sometimes never knew who we had or why, it was some grey area you sometimes hear about. The 'need to know' factor. Didn't need to know, we never did ask. If it were a dead man, why know them in the first place, it seemed easier. To not know them was to stay just far enough away to where it wouldn't bother so bad if they were taken down. That's not where it ended either, there was rolls of paperwork following any event, and if it wasn't one of our guys, then it seemed they were gone quicker. Some of the new tools wanted to know who they were dealt sometimes; they were always the curious.

Never mattered.

Chapter 6

When the soldiers marched through the house, we were gone. Nobody kept to the side or stayed behind to see them. We all found places to rest out from time. Our homes became cold. Towards the west we'd heard stories, of a great rift, a savage anger against soldiers. When our times became diminished and we kept a warm sun on our backs, it took a strong will and determination to gather and turn, and to leave. Running, Pierce threw down behind the front tire, blocked in against the wind and snow.

"Take him out!" Kate's radio crackled.

"You shoot. Pierce, use your head and take cover, shoot," she whispered.

Cover or what, wait? Pierce could see her moving a foot and leg, turning as to pull and roll.

"Bamm!"

Floyd keyed in, "...one down."

"Okay take your shot."

"I did" she said.

Pierce cleared the sweep of the upper overhead walkway and parking lot. "Anyone else you want to shoot today Kate?"

"Pierce, you make me run this back."

A dark red syrup filled cracks in the old pavement. His twisted arm and leg seemed to be running in the other direction to the rest of him. Pierce slowly nudged a belt-line only making sure time had stopped under the fallen weight. Once its undone, things are changed. It can't all be good. Sticky spots dripped along the back wall where he'd tried to run to get away. All of the sudden, just by chance he'd thought a clearer picture appeared.

Three large laundry bags, a tanned grey and brown leather belt wrapped tightly around. Where he'd missed searching, their emergence rote before his eyes. There everything was.

Chapter 7

It was a still morning. He watched as a tan-yellow brown moth flutter up the bedroom wall, its batting wings full and fluffy. The moth's vertical ascent to the top and back was an art in motion. Up and down next to the green painted wall. It would drop down and touched its bottom mid-fall, and then flutter there. Then up again, shimmering to another different place. Touch that dot and back down. Rhythm or not, the fuzz-bomb set a soft pace to his plans. Comm truck, more importantly his positions. They'd be in place at the accurate times, now only a phone call and the fall freeze coming.

Refreshed, wrestling away from sleep, he'd have done as his father in the darkness of the early days. The morning light bounced away, and some rigid energy-rays drilling down and deep into Terra. They had traveled four hours at light-speed. From the crescents of another waning fall moon, it always seemed as though Pierce's destinations were seldom without friends and danger.

Early before shades of any new crepuscular light asks human-kind to rejoin again into what had become the symphonies of life, mother re-sends her message. Whisked away from gallows by the energies of our sun, standing and moving he looks out and over the patches of dust-land searching from one to the other horizon, he even once tried to see past into the depths of the waves of signaling time. Dusk to dawn stretched away as resurgence called him to post.

Yes, it was frustrating. A sensible dedication to a humble sim-plicity painted a big 'detour' signal clearly in his pathway. Fred knew everything and still crumbled. Running along any possible 'wow-signal' road on the march of life, he was walking in a requiem.

Between this time and what was the past and any solutions derived from problems, his workroom contained solutions, and tools. Flexible solutions, and solid rain. He was finding time though all corners taken to be at a quiet safety zone.

Pierce's rock garden saw a bit of time too. An unusual cold would flow in toward joining patches of the dusty dirt. Swirls of dust, weightless in motion, shaded green moss edges along the bottom inch. He would catch up with stereo-radios and Dairy Queen ice-cream signs, but he was just a small, skinny-framed kid, and took to riding along in front, rolling the car window down and sticking his arm out to catch the breeze and to wave.

Wiser than rocks, and browned by the dust, they kept driving.

There was San Pedro.

The way there? He thought he knew, and Fred? He was well, more experienced. He'd traveled as his job then.

Continents.

"I'd search for any solution to any problem, and you need patience." he often said.

"Time and tools." he said to his young son.

"See it? It's a '66."

He'd imagined the thing, never seen a picture, even less ever held one. Just as the newspaper ad was written, there it was! Sugar wrapped Golden Brown. A single round mirror, a black interior with cool "Nip & Tuck" upholstery, and a big steering wheel.

Pierce kept seeing flashbacks from that old TV show "My Mother the Car".

"Are you certain this is it, the one? A little old looking," he remarked, "is that dust or just the color?"

"Yes, this is it."

A guy was either a Ford man or drove a Chevy. An El Camino would cost much more, that was his first choice. He'd seen a black one once, two red strips covering the hood, but no other would have done. Except then Plymouth Chargers started running around. Challengers, Mustangs, Corvettes, station wagons and vans, they were all more than he'd saved so far.

Eyes gleamed.

He could just about see inside this one, driving around the station and later to Rocky's Hamburger place. Up and back so all the girls would see him and maybe talk, or point. Rolling back windows and parking with his best friends, putting both seats back to recline. One comment and then some girl's sister would come over, looking for answers. Drive-In movie, steam soaked windows, back seat ravishment. All possibilities were open.

"Okay, let's do some talking, see how much he'll take," Fred said.

There were no discussions, no second opinions. What was right was right. The ritual of buying his first car had commenced, and Pierce listened speechless. A goal, a major turning point along the invisible paths of modern life. Crawling to stand, walking to run, riding a bicycle then motor scooter. The energy of change froze him into a worried, uncertain and weird bystander in the noisy cacophony of sixteen years of pent-up experiences.

His dad was pretty cool and sharp, his business acuity was only the first drop in the bucket. They watched as the old guy motioned to his son. Both hands in his pocket, his discomfort in the conversations were too obvious.

"We want to see how much you'll take for that car, what's bottom price?"

"Well, I'm at what I put on the newspaper ad, no less."

Pierce looked at the young guy, then at the old man, then back at his dad.

"Uh, can I get a drive around?" They couldn't believe what he'd said, what stupid thing he'd blasted off. Not normal from the young teen, a micron of an older person longing to live freely. To be cool and to buy a car, that wasn't easy or was it? Another minute, then another and another. Slowly, as the shifting continuum of endless time slipped by and his weight shifted back to his other leg, he heard the winds, felt the cool snap breeze past his skinny bones. Some leaves in trees blinked at him. He looked back at it again. A paint job!

Everything started moving. The old man was saying something to the kid, pointing inside the car and then at the wheels. A 5-spoke black aluminum, with a classic G60 Peerless Sprint GT, set flat to ground on both sides, made for the race-strip. A preacher and practical, fairly new. He breathed-in to taste the smell of new rubber. Two door coupe, the cinnamon brown brick, with a muscular set of tires and wheels.

A quick look inside again, he moved toward the front, "So, what's she got?"

Young guy stuck a hand in his blue-jeans jacket pocket, pulled out something tied to a key. With slow hesitation and moving about center of the front, he reached into the slotted aluminum grill, found a pad lock, and slipped the key in.

"Click, thunk. Cah-jenke, cah-jenke," from the links of chain dropping under the hood of the car. Then he moved, "Ca-clink, clunk."

In a split motion the hood lock opened the safety hook released. An indescribable but impressive beauty appeared as it went up. He pulled the loose chain links up top, then dropped the weight on the frame. Shiny chrome polished pipes, a cool alternator and custom fan, a tarantula manifold, big carb and and an open air-cleaner. Everything else was like magic. Cleaned pipes swept down to disappear back underneath the engine and new black water hoses and a big battery stuck out. Four thick red wires on both sides curled over to the top to a black-top rotor. It looked fast, and the chromed front bumper left no overkill for insects and birds. He stepped back, a highly modified engine torqued down between two skinny front tires.

"Well, is this the car you wanted?"

"Yes."

"Give him twenty-two hundred and its yours," the older man said.

An argument seemed about to ensue. There was whiskery-talking, back and forth, and at one point the young dude-kid stomped a boot in the dust and tightly clenched both fists.

Fletcher stood fast, folded arms and a firm gaze on his prodigy that held moments of crispy matter of fact which we had not known yet existed.

"Remember our agreement, your words."

"Yes sir."

"We talked about this."

"I know, and you are right, but I worked hard."

"You learned, you know."

Young dude was barely over a hundred and twenty pounds standing up. Two sacks of gardening dirt. Not much more than a hungry mouth to feed, and all the hope and dreams the old man had.

"Now get your stuff out of the car and take his money."

"But it's not enough!"

"It's enough and more."

"So, what if I don't want to sell it?"

"We made a 'Man' agreement, we agreed."

By now young dude was about exhausted, almost ready to cry. He looked over at his car and kicked up the dusty clump of dirt he'd slowly piled up talking. Noises from the street began again, swooping branches moved. He kept pulling at the string and key, dangling it from his fist. They could all see his panic, the eagerness of eminent loss dashed to ragged rocks. He couldn't let go of the key. All the young man's planning detoured. The shiny key eventually to be lost anyway. Fletcher's jacket fluttered as a warm breeze whooshed around. Those guided muse's hands pushing the future at us. Another time lost, to the age of innocence, times when we knew so much.

Pierce look at him, then the old man. He looked back at his dad.

So far as they could ever hope, it's more likely most people would all have title to a car someday. Earlier, Fred had stopped at one of a handful of used-car lots. Prices ranged from not much to way too much. After passing one and then another, they turned in, stopped and parked. Doors opened and they looked. Couple of large station wagons. Unmoved, he kept his back to the office as Pierce walked further out into the gravel lot, searching for a nice white two door. The big sign on the office trailer window spelled "Low Mileage, V8 Clean" and while they knew some salesperson was probably on the way, Pierce kept looking. Finally, Fred tracked him down anyway and broke the ice with a "Hey, welcome to Hardin's Used cars" and shook hands, made some finger points and mutter about a small white cake. Some of the humming from Hardin's mechanic's open-air garage froze and the air compressor's "tooch, tooch, toossch" sound slowly stopped.

"Call me Larry!"

He made points with Fred saying he owned four cars already and he wasn't even married. The quick look out into the lot had said no anyway. Curiously, he watched from behind a cleaned up 2-door Plymouth Fury III, as it seemed Fred was enjoying the idea of owning so many cars, and also the parts about not being married, and then only quietly asking about it.

The car.

Turning back around, Pierce looked over at young dude again, probably not much older maybe about seven or eight years. He looked destined to work on cars forever at that garage for his dad. Not even sure that that much money was enough for all the freedom and responsibility of owning a real car meant. Driving without hesitation, going places he'd only recently heard about. And camp outs.

He put all the cash he'd stuffed into his pocket on the hood of that car and counted.

Chapter 8

The screen door slammed behind him as he walked out into the bright, sunny day. Looking at the compass he had tied to a pants-loop, he sighted which direction North and made 37 paces, stopping at the corn field and turned. Along the way and before long he'd lost sight of his house, and as we could say, was on his way.

Cutting through back yards, and crossing one street and some driveways, he walked along hearing birds chirping and the dogs at the house with the tall long white fence barking. Rustles of leaves in the trees muffled the car sounds and a distant clump of trees and bushes showed him the outline of the little town he called home.

"Grown-ups," he thought to himself.

He remembered the two sandwiched he'd brought and so quickly stuffed into his green backpack and the spaghetti he'd ate yesterday. After two extra servings, the French toasted bread and some candy treat afterward, the big red apple in his pants pocket seemed only an excuse to remember what his dad had said.

"Going somewhere?"

"Well maybe. Mom and you told me I'd have to leave someday. So, I think I'll go now and then be back sooner." Martin said.

"You need to pack if you're going."

"I know."

"Mother is going to miss her boy."

"She will? What? I haven't really decided to leave yet."

"That's what moms do. They worry about their little indians. How long are you expecting to be gone?"

"Dad, I'm six'n and not a kid anymore. I'll be seven in four days and can to go to California, to be a real cowboy."

"Be a cowboy? You don't have… to go to California to be a cowboy." His father gave him a tough face look, "Well, we'll see."

Martin clenched his fists and folded his arms, then stomped a foot on the wooden floor. "But Dad!"

By then his mother's tears wet his cheek as he hugged both and said goodnight.

Chapter 9

He'd woke up that day and lifted out from his bed. As he jumped into pants and eagerly tied shoestrings, he even remembered the compass from cub scouts and tied it to his belt.

He was a bit lonely as he walked, trying to break away from the entanglement of a rural life. As Martin crossed a small creek, he stumbled, and landed in some mucky mud soaking his shoes and socks. His trousers were splashed with the sticky goo. As he brushed, it smeared everywhere. Feeling the joy for once, he felt happy not to hear his little sister, or his mother telling him things like to pick up the toys. Taking out the garbage or sweeping was okay, but cleaning his room made no sense.

The neighbors' dogs would never bark at him, and over the creek bank across the big field they followed. From there he could see a big red barn. Only a few more miles maybe. After sloshing forward in wet shoes, and what seemed like many miles, and running, he experienced the death march from what he thought was about half a mile. Running was strenuous exercise which changed the adventure into something like heavy lifting, and the dogs barking and chasing some kind of animal, and an empty water canteen.

The red barn, which seemed quite small from a distance, it loomed over him while his eyes slowly adjusted to the shadows. He found a door and slipped in just before the rain drops sprinkled outside and the quiet 'plink, plink-plink' metallic noises from the roof filled the huge open barn space. The two hound dogs sniffed around and found places to lay down.

Startled by the sound of a horse in the greyed-out room, the air thickened and tickled his nose. He was able to breath quick short breathes, acknowledging the horse smell. As day light faded outside, some soft horse muffles created a cozy feeling inside the old barn.

"Over here."

He stood up looking around curiously not believing if he heard something or somebody was there. Moving around the thought of what he heard might have been the horse for some reason, he kept looking around.

Almost panicky, he had the sense there was no place to hide and seemed lost in the deep dark barn as he looked. Slowly, the grayness faded as his eyes began to adjust and he saw the outlines of old steps and the loft scattered with straw. The smoky light filtered in as he could barely make out a set of stalls and the silhouette against the slat-boarded side of the barn. Standing in a roped off square stall was a very big horse.

"Over here."

There it was…again. The muffled sounds came from the horse.

"Scared?"

He looked around for the door again. He couldn't run now he was frozen and scared out of his pants. Turning back, he saw the creature. It wasn't a little horse, it was a big, huge one. Darkness shadowed the hooves and four muscular legs. It bowed its big head and raised a big nose and pushed some air out from its big nose and lips.

"Pbbooooshh!"

Martin rubbed both his eyes, gathered the courage, and moved slowly toward the big steed as its tremendous weight shifted from one set of legs to the other. Martin shook his head and punched himself as he quietly inched closer and looked into the big dark eyes of the giant brown animal. As he caught himself balancing with one hand on the side of the stall, the horse motioned in the straw.

"Can you talk?" he asked watching as she nodded and stuck her nose out. His eyes widened and he stepped back.

"Of course, I can ppbooosch talk."

"But I'm a boy!" Martin said. "And a hunter, a indian and some-day I'll be a cowboy. I can camp out and make traps and catch animals. I can climb trees and play baseball too. And hike and do anything a girl can do except better. Are you a boy horse?"

"Neahhh."

"Oh well, do you eat a sandwich, do you want some sandwich?"

Silence.

"Oh yeah, I almost forgot, eat some straw." Then, reaching out he gathered a large bundle of the dried straw and pushed it in front of his new friend as she took a munching bite. He couldn't believe she talked. Martin was pretty good at talking and he'd been in a spelling contest at school. He talked his way out of a fight with Larry the stupid bully the time he'd went over to his house to get back his bike that he stole. He could listen pretty well to dad when he talked about work and how to weld and when mom made those silly noises to his little sister all the time which he just tried to ignore, but he hadn't talked to a horse before.

"Cowboy huh?"

"Yeah" he said almost boasting. "I'm headed west to rope cows and camp, build cook fires, and eat chick-peas from the chuck-wagon, and beans and ..." Martin was thinking about the sandwiches, and not believing he had heard what he heard so he asked, "what kind of horse did you say you are anyways?"

"Ppbbhh."

This wasn't going easily. "Um, maybe a plow horse? Are you a plow horse?"

She turned her head and looked Martin square in the eyes. Not saying anything this time, she turned back to eating the straw.

"Well did you want to go with me?" He asked. "We could find some friends or someplace and we could build a camp and yeah, you could be my horse and...you could run...and I...and I could name you." It didn't matter what ever kind of horse it was, he could ride any horse even if it could talk. He looked up at the hat with two cut outs though the top hanging on the wall.

"Oh! Okay, well do you know how to get to California from here?"

She motioned toward the barn doors shaking her head up and down sideways then swished her tail.

"Right, just…ok, and what's your name?"

"Pbboosh, Polly!"

She reached for more straw, as he pulled the old fisherman's hat over her ears and tossed the leather strap back around her neck.

"How does this go, anyway," he thought.

He'd fastened the leather like he had seen on TV once while his little fingers struggled with the silvery buckle to hook. He struggled three times throwing a blanket over before it landed just right. His arms pulled and smoothed it out as she watched with her great big eyes. Martin pulled the rope over to one side and held tight as she swished her tail and clop-clopped out into the open area inside.

"Can you ride?"

"Of course, I can ride," Martin said. "Do you have to teach a cowboy how to pull on his boots?"

With that he stacked two wooden Coke crates and jumped up on top. Slowly she moved next to the boy and the stack of crates. Holding one leg up, he jumped across her back, holding tight to the mane.

"Almost jumped too far, see?"

"Think we could go outside, maybe?"

"Yeah, that's the idea."

"Forget your pack?"

"Just let me get down, and we get on." Leaning over he hugged her, slid down and ran to the knapsack with the food. His compass fell out and with one quick stoop motion he scooped it up and stuffed it in his pants pocket. Running to cola crates he tugged and motioned her move back. She felt his weight and leaned to the big door, nudging it open with a flat nose as he pulled on the strap. Moving past an old rusty hay baler, rain sprinkles stopped and the warm sun made dew drops glisten. They slowly moved down the old country road.

Chapter 10

Day 2, lost.

"Hey where were ya headed there?"

"Just up the road, west, to open prairie and river canyons".

"Hey kid, you Marson?"

"My dad, his is Marson."

Well, I'll be, and you say you goin' Californie?"

That's right how did you know that?"

"Well, heard on the radio, last night, about you and said you'd be out this way. They said you're going west! Ahhh, to let you know everyone was praying for you. Do you need some hep?"

"No, sir thanks. Just could you tell me which way is west? I think I turned at the bridge and couldn't see back any.

"Um ok, sure, let's see," the old farmer in blue overalls gasped. He scratched the grey beard and patted Polly as he walked around. A big corn field on the right side with two-foot shoots fogged out into the green morning steam. "If you go back over the bridge, near the old railroad track, uh, the tracks and follow them oh, about a mile you'll get about past a big corn field see. Cross through the field, stay between them rows and when you git to the road, you see Jenkin's store. Go past there, an' ah, road'll cut back over to the river. Uh, stay on the road and you get to cement, and a wood bridge over the river. Cross over, go out the other side closest alongside where the cement road starts again, but stay on the trail. See your way?"

He looked up at him, a silver sparkle from his eyes caught in glance.

"You said about a mile, and then field and then what?"

"Yeah, that's it. Um well, needin some company see you through?"

"Not sure if I can find the trail, but that's okay, you can go too, if you think your mom won't never bother any."

"Yeah, really be keen, we can all go, you, me and Polly."

"Who's Polly?" The old farmer asked.

"She's my horse, tell him Polly."

Polly looked up at the old farmer with the blue overalls and long grey beard, and shook her head from side to side, "Pbshhh."

"Come on girl talk to him." Martin said.

"She can't talk, no horse can talk."

"Yes, she can, she told me her name and about some kids who like to take her around."

"Well, I'll be, when was all that?"

"Over in the barn where I found her. What's your name mister?"

"The big red barn? The one back over the hill two miles?"

"Yes sir."

The old farmer in the blue overalls with the grey beard looked up at Martin and then back to the old brown horse as she reached through the fence, nibbling at the long shoots of blue grass.

"Got food?"

Martin smiled and reached into the pack and pulled out one and the other half of smashed peanut butter jelly sandwich. He pulled off half and asked, "Hey mister, what's your name?"

"Schmidt."

"You mean old man Schmidt?"

Martin started talking about Indians and hunting as they walked along and made up a story about catching a rabbit once, set up a wire trap and was roasting it in a campfire when they jumped in and took all his rabbit meat. And then, shooting an arrow and by luck getting another one and cooked it and that the meat tasted so good and that he was full of hunting any more rabbits.

Old man Schmidt talked to Martin about the midnight attack on the old settler's fort from "them indians" once, and war paint and when he could hear them calling "com…ouu…, com…oouuut". Even when everyone in the camp was sleeping, how they did "com-out", out from the lost underground caves and surrounded settlers' camp. His eyes widened, and then he started in about the ghost of the stolen horse. In a German accent, he told Martin about the long arrows, and when Indians shot into the canvas covered wagon as he watched them, lighting the sky as they arced across and caught fire where it cut the covers.

"What old fort? You mean real Indians?"

"Yeah, right here. They would hunt down by the creek. Found some good arrows, und good collection now."

"Some arrows?"

"You come to see."

"Really, can I?"

"Mom! Look . . . over here! I'm here! Look at the horse I found. Can I keep her? Don't worry Polly, my room is next to the back yard, and I'll keep you and take good care of you.

"Oh Mr. Smith, he couldn't cause any trouble."

 "Mom?"

"No Miss, he can visit the old girl whenever he cans."

"Or perhaps, but first his father will see him this evening. Not sure if, but will he take a stick to him. Martin, hope that your father doesn't."

"Please, the company, we are good company. We go back up to the barn." He brushed her side and big neck and pulled at the harness strap. They moved up the path to the big field. The old farmer in the blue overalls and the big old horse looked back to see Martin waving.

"Der good kinder, that Marte."

"Neaah…"

"Think he'll be back to see you, Polly?"

"Bebeeshh," she said, swishing her tail and clip-clopping up the dusty brown path.

Chapter 11

2/21 Williamsport, PA

So, we were to deter.

That started at the park.

After coming down from off Lay-hill road, we cruised up to speed, and there they were under trap-caps. Almost um-obvious. Then, I don't know how they will react to radar after all the toy stores were gone and the buildings torn down. Pierce began when experiences were expenses and time, not even enough of it, remained for them to live then.

Live man song.

Life when I'm away,
let's go there.

I'd like
a world of change,
make me
appreciate those dreams.

Let love
to explain all I have,
let's go there.

Take these dreams and make them mine

~ Cream "Higher"

He looked at him while he cleared the deceased victim.

"Pierce, what are you trying to find on him. Let's clear and have them do returns."

His attention did not stop.

"Okay."

"Do I do anything for nothing. So then ask, do you speed across what time alone creates, and if you do then account for it, somehow?"

By then, not finding any clear direction our assignment had taken, he stayed silent.

"Two, I would pray and see the Lord, as I haven't contacts nor anyone outside other than my neighbor, who would I share this with?"

Pierce spread the jacket pocket open pulling a small wallet and radio from him.

"They are accountable to themselves."

"Explain this."

"What?"

"You are a nobody. A true nothing. You travel because they let you. You go where they want and use a system for free yet, you're a guard with your life. You are tested and held accountable Sans Reproach; integrity bound. And not made guilty and certainly never accused of doing a wrong."

"Why do any of it? Take the risk rolled up in big boat load of goo?"

He stared out and back to the dead body. As he stood up and pointed at me, he said, "No, I am not the Outlaw."

Chapter 12

7/2/79 - Grand Island, NE

The Bandit

Angel "Blanco" McDermot stood up and walked to the window at the sheriff's office overlooking the county court buildings.

"Fellows, the outlaw finds no rest, and someone waits for him to ever make any wrong move."

"The Judas seeker," someone yelled up from outside!

"There he is! Get him! Make him pay!" They all yelled up all together, the mob decided at an instant that he was destined to rot in a ravine of human waste as ever there would be a place for him to rest. They only viewed him as an un-human form of waste.

A sudden quiet hushed the crowd. It was him, they'd all noticed a smallish person being led down and past the front steps. With even quickness, they walked past four or six people waving and yelling, and at another step down, he looked up over at the window, and walked to exit at the street sidewalk. Somebody with a mic and a cameraman walking up stopped them.

"Are you the man they say, did you see him?'

"I am who followed Jesus, I am seeking him. I know that scorn against me from long ago. They have murdered me time and time again. They have hanged me and cut through my neck. They suffocated me and strangled my dreams and hope. This is who I am if I am he, if I were not a bandit from a long time past."

The crowd parted away and out. Witnesses give way for them to walk to the black SUV.

Chapter 13

2/25 - Pleasant View, WI.

Only a short bit of time had passed.

"I'm home," he said, "and in no way anticipating a long journey like on the road."

Pierce's living partner kept relatively busy while he was away. She kept to her schedule, uncertain whenever he'd return sometimes.

"What will tomorrow...?"

She heard his voice from the bathroom he kept. Sinking to the back kitchen pantry corner she searched for the can of soup she picked out at a grocer from the other day.

"Shower with me?"

And, again she faintly recognized his voice over the blasting music on the stereo system. Why try to run but, she wanted to sometimes and again her young heart screamed. A simple screen door kept her from dashing while she tiptoed by, fainting back, she hurriedly crouched down against the warm humming refrigerator, two fingers scratching at the paper can label wrap.

"I'm waiting now."

An epic romantic rascal, she recalled him the last time he'd passed through. Now praying for an open afternoon dispatch, she was slowly thinking that faking head aches wouldn't deter him. She moved slowly while the music played.

Slowly as the song ended and moved to a Sunny California commercial, he sat up from soaking in bubbly warm water. Brushing water and his jet-black hair back, the young agent reached for a bottle of water.

"The time home swooshes by you see, as if our fates are suspended, only just for that little bit of a while, you know, whenever you, well my … anyway, think about it."

Never fazed how quickly hours had passed. Why only three whole days, why not four? In a field, practicing. He thought about the field in France, spelling farewells to a lonesome lover, both with distant lives to live out. Probably, if not for certain.

Pierce was traveling east again. Fun traveling through time and images. He sped along, passed them he did so quickly. Quicker than if he could describe any of it to anyone.

Hundreds of thousands of people and times, epic blurred images of wander. Some sunsets shadows caste far ahead out away from him, they'd race up the next mountain hill while he'd see if he would get to there any faster.

He was not there, never.

I remembered what it was we were thinking about. Some kinds of mountain tops, big grey wolves, and the streaky yellow haze across the skies.

Chapter 14

2/26 Green Bay, WI.

A core-chilling cold buried life all around.

"And this is who I am."

An old farmer stared up at him with one eye squeezed closed against the bright sun light.

"But I don't know who you are."

"No, you are not who you say you are."

"I am me, while you are," he said, "you aren't much, uh mostly nothing, a nobody."

All this while not a single word dampened the morning air. Pierce moved slowly down.

Crunching and cracking, liken to smooth frozen cloth, it moved like a big dead snake, unbending, not even straightened. At the end it knotted in a loop fashioned for a tow strap, and as it cleared the ice and hooked on, he grabbed up to the front while keeping from slipping back. He could see light and heard the clip, and in a half second flipped the safety, and pulled.

Without another look, the engine revved up to full power and the old man waved as if saying it had been a long time and breakfast was getting cold. Lurching forward, and then back again, he heard the first ping.

"Ho."

"Hold it, wait," the old farmer yelled back. He sat bent over the steering wheel and pushing the gear into second. Against cold and winds, his farm tractor slid a few inches and stopped. The left side wedged in by the edge of road and grunting as the engine power began pulling at the big black brick.

"Err-errr, bajunk, bah-jeunk, errrrch, bajeunk." Pulling and then backing, all four of the large SUV's wheels sank, both front wheels spinning as they eased back deep into chalky ruts.

"Clear."

Pierce looked over and up, the two crosshair marks set square on.

Did he tell you a dream or just another fantasy of lonesome freedom? You choose. He chose. He won't try to transcribe it, so his writings long to cure some part of him. He was many people many times, not an outlaw nor the bandit. You are not the same.

Chapter 15

3/3 Mountain Home, MT.

Remember now.

When he told.

He spoke to you of high desert mountains and out rocks carved
by the winds of time. Recall all the purples. All the mornings lit by
the red sage high up in cold range mountains.

Feel the coolness of day as you awaken, let the sun warm your
face, turn to the southern skies from inside some morning shade
hideaway.

Watch the eagle soar along closest to you, their cool loose flex-
ing wings searching under reflecting green river rapids in a twisted
past. It swoops then, and dives down with claws stretched. Hunter
eyes, no hesitating doubt no boasts of shear-sharp talons splashing
up, scaled prey and away, a fish wiggling that grey midair dance
around death.

Today, a warm hue embraced you while another rises and lifts
your soul. Where great soaring cliff shadows hang, an eagle taken
in crisp heating boils up away past rocky edges. Bathe heated blue-
bleached heights.

It won't be too long, we see birds again.

"Yes, we must."

Chapter 16

3/9 Petersburg, VA.

As its gone and looked back, we've laughed and cried and didn't think when it just might ever cease. Pierce sees his passed journeys through times when I could only wonder how blessed it was to be there and alive.

Even when lost traveling out, he let to reason.

Where he was away, he's there, where he is.

And when away, I'm still here, where I am. I can't get anywhere without still being this, it can not change.

Even the warming sun feels as though it's kept me here.

But no, when it's cold and the wind rocks that big black boat, don't want to be here. Let the bow turn sideways on a lonesome frozen forty-foot wave and see who gets swept away. We're still going, shoulders tucked against the cold northeast wind.

Chapter 17

3/18 Norfolk, NE. 6,121

Though weather turns, ponds are froze solid now, some birds are out. Frightful winds push and pull my launch across a river's dead current, back and forth. Pierce, he sees them getting swept away, seemingly struggling to reach some other side, to some other survival. As some endless invisible wind pushes worn-out black wings against what nature wills, some perch along wire fences, here and there, frozen. Tucked down on winded branch, snow covered backs bent away from bleak chills. Even a prophet prays, but only to walk along the edges of the civilized warmth.

He knew that.

An anchor in time, something to believe in.

Where were the times when a black boat didn't seem lost.

"Eh, you going in?"

The voice was that old man's voice. His thick smokey words like piles driven down into some thickened muddy shore. He was standing back toward the storm outside an entrance to a midtown diner, a walk-in to vanilla soda-fountain milkshakes and french-fry plates. For seconds he stood there, both hands wrapped in thick gloves. A hooded overcoat and scarf wrapped on his head, he held a brown leather coat fast to his body. Quiet as night, the old-timer turned and walked into the sliver of reflections in the door as he disappeared.

He was nearly forever watching him before walking off. A white silvery frost began to cover the windows and front hoods. The darkest cup of coffee couldn't chase the grey that day. He looked and looked for signs of her returning, only to see shooting stars across a thick empty sky.

"You had pressure."

"Remember, no pressure?"

All that you need, what you wanted was all left for good.

Chapter 18

3/20 Wye, MT

This had to be another day filled with unexpected experiences and frustration. It is shameful to have to produce writings of the bad side of an existence. About twenty or thirty miles out of town you can find them. The open areas, they needed these kinds of stops for the lost and long distance runners. This is only somewhat true and many ingredients of distance driver lives have changed, it is part of our world.

A stop is just that, nothing more. Worn out and rusted tin sided buildings needing paint. Older stops are worse. Decades of filth have taken over in some rooms. Corners of the convenience store and driver supply shelves fade into darkened aisles. The newness to some places has worn away as busy times seemingly existed within these ruins only a short day ago. Open twenty-four hours now, they maybe were closed soon after sunset, maybe only a wrecker driver due for some late night rescue. Almost every runner out today has wandered inside those places.

St. Regis wasn't any different. To think a runner wouldn't care. If he doesn't care then who will? Not to expect one or two people to loath care to hundreds every day. Its like a baseball game with only small home-run victories against those who would be their muse. Back twenty-four miles to Paradise, and making the turn around at an OK Cafe Casino and a diner. Holding on to his black boat and trailer, they made the run and drove them back down to Belgrade. Stopping most of twenty minutes before turning back up to inter-state and fixing the cruise control at 80, now it was on into the Wye and to De Smet, a federal detention site at the Hamlet listed as a first drop. He slowed down to stop.

That restaurant, and that cheap silver and the so small buffet all had a strong appeal. Certainly perhaps fried chicken and maybe a meatloaf been out. The smell of a smoldered out cigarette was in the stale air, and six black leather counter stools stood in resign under an amber light. Pierce heard the waitress call for another breakfast.

"Two eggs, bacon, and biscuits gravy."

Out the side of one eye he watched her move toward a coffee maker and listening closely, he could hear another unbelievable by the chance fascinating story being told. Some eager youngster's ear listening.

Looking through the dusty window out over the yard, deep ruts and potholes in the parking lot spattered muddy water puddles and some blue-oily runoffs. The fuel island smeared grimy diesel, the soldiery pumps but looked standing assuredly at attention. The filler handle worn and bent still worked. They were named, those tireless machines, but only for keeping working.

"Tomorrow is coming, it will be here soon too."

Another ship arrived and it begins all over. Listen as another traveler pauses past us.

Pierce did not really want to eat. but a waitress catches him as he begins to leave, he's surly trying to spend as little time and money in the place.

He grunts "tea and no sugar," and flops back into the worn booth with the phone stuck to the wood panel. Suddenly, a menu floats across on the table in front of him.

Her big eyes, her eyebrows smoothed like the wings of a hawk. He could tell from her glance back on him, by her didn't care if its raining or snowing look, and only by her thinks she can fly hair style that she fits in.

He pause and then, "Um, hey didn't I tell you about the mountains and sandy rock cliffs? The winds?"

"Oh, last time, whenever you knocked over the fuel stand out there, got it all over in here and we told you to leave and never come back?"

She smirked as she looked through the window searching for the mountain sages turned purple higher up, where the cold snaps and you feel the pull of darkness on your shoulders.

"Will it surprise you? Come away and run with me."

A warm hue enveloped her as she pulled away. Thoughts about cliffs, where he'd whispered about eagles soaring.

"They reached to the sky and they floated, we'll see those birds again."

"You go see them."

She returned with a paper and laid it at the end of the table. He noticed the name tag pinned on her sweater as she dropped the bags of tea into his cup and filled it with hot water.

"Joni," he said, "you're free and young, you can leave here, find some other place to take up. Go with me a while and you'll see."

"Rigger, if that's what you're calling yourself today, would you stop off here for a day, and we'll go up to Saint Mary's Lake, its about an hours drive from the Hamlet."

She turned the kettle up to stop the hot water and looked into the pocket of her blue apron and then back at Pierce.

"Are you ready for me? Do you know how free I need to be?" She moved back away from him and looked at the two kitchen doors. Her apron strings swaying from side to side as she floated away, past the fountain through the doors to the kitchen.

The first time he'd stopped, a short man with sad sunken cheek bones and awful bad breath and worn out jeans warned Pierce. Someone had talked to him. The place was different now, it felt smaller, colorless and cold. The silence of that early morning had stirred his gut and his neck hair raised when he caught his first breathe. She had hurried past him, given a half smile and looked to the tray of left-over dishes. She was like a bird. She'd landed here and there, and fluttered around the diner with her little arms.

He watched her as she turned a cowboy around and told him he couldn't be stinking in her place, anytime or anyway. He watched over to some other tables and across the counter. In Kansas he thought...

"Are you dreaming?"

"No, I really don't want to eat anything, uhm," he tried to ask, "can you tell me, what have you seen Joni? In the mountains, the streams and the deep rivers?" and like a strong wind, she moved towards him a step.

"How strange was it, the times which may have been and the things that never were?"

Flashes of smiling faces and those times he thought were.

It's almost midnight, and cold.

Chapter 19

3/22 Intercession City, FL

Another car passes, the palm-trees lined out evenly alongside a long dry white pavement.

Cars pass along, each one has its own distinct sounds as hot winds whip over and around those rolling metal ovens.

"Sir Richard wrote, to listen to you again."

How does it seem when it isn't a single car passing. The rising east warmth softened a road into Campbell. He hears as another one comes. It's away, up off in the distance, faint at first. Then a fuzzy "humming" of a gleaming aircraft, its singular approach, louder and louder, nearer as it glides above rocky sand banks, slower. As if its hovering aloft to sense life, to analyze all the variables and all the present knowns. Chips blindly oscillating spelling out blinking colorless soundings until finally it passes, on away. Overhead, and then away and the noises fade, they go down, then off into a past and on into all the nothingness.

He will not look, they all appear the same in the darkness, those shiny lights and silvery reflections.

Blurs of the people, white clamped fists on control wheels, and little noses flattened against back seat windows, they all are looking, peering out, searching to see whatever was.

He would not have pity for them, but he felt a subtle weight of envy mostly, not angry envy, as it shows its ignorance, not any impartial truth.

He's one though Pierce hardly admits the same.

Chapter 20

3/31 Knoxville, TN

Keep looking.

Ah, exit sixty-two.

There, here, turn here, this is it, it's the one.

It's the one here, yes. Turn, turn, okay ease off and feel the load slowing. He'd been searching for a while. To refuel and rest. Here is where life gets harder, his little bits of faith and energy left in the day.

He was down. Walking along hurriedly, a little sick and this was all he could get together to write? Pierce was not about to be sick while out on the road, that only made everything worse.

A year ago, Steve downed some spoiled ketchup, he ended up along a side of the road heaving at the woods.

Harder to concentrate and rest, now they weren't taking depositions to get any extra rest. He felt better and healthy last week, only now he could have a potato, a full Ketchup bottle, and coffee.

Back then, he'd had more time to burn more energy, and so instead of waiting, he found parking and walked over up into the buildings. Security guard here but not always, and never the same. A missed convergence due to a misaligned schedule had the weirdness of being in front of another Fed a perpetual drainage of thought. He needed to eat but couldn't stomach it. Maybe breakfast would be good, a bite would do for a bit.

He found cough drops, and coffee again.

Another full tank for the final push down into Ft. Worth, Pierce dropped his seat down and into lock, set the cruiser to 140.

Chapter 21

4/6 Dallas, TX

When Steve talked about a life running, and his need to take responsibility as time goes, all those discussion roads follow along and out to another and another, on into that endless sun-setting skyline drawn onto the faces of castaways and dirges. Peachy orange clouds and the vast open prairie stretched way out in front. That was where his forbidden towns and city streets lay in wait, waiting for childish innocence to tackle the days.

Nothing changes.

It's all still the same, the cold asphalt hardened by the passing of time. Flat out, casting no shadow.

A place to hide?

Everywhere we go, they've taken away the sides of roads, isn't a place to stop anymore.

Assigned to pick up someone out west, first Pierce hoped to stretch out and hear those sounds of solitude. The quiet of a half-moon night wildly surrounding his earthbound time, and it tried creeping in on him again. All those doors surely locked, windows drawn up as far as could be. And what?

She never knew he would not feel safe buried in his bed. Sometimes, any sounds he heard were suspect, and some would have him bound up to look out and to see, if only he could see.

Chapter 22

4/8 Tucson, AZ

No one out there. A few trees swaying with thick heated winds. Cardboard boxes and paper cups moved across the street in front. To the east a hazy lit sky.

"I spent some time wondering where he'd be next week."

"No uncertainty in that."

A stronger breeze rocked the black boat, enough to make him sleepy. Steve always figured perhaps in maybe a couple hours traffic would die out.

Angel grew tired and slipped back to search for sleep.

What will it be tonight? How about Vienna sausage and crackers, a warm soda pop, cough drops, and for desert those two gelcaps. As he turned over to fall into deep rest, thoughts drifted to the images from that day, of the two sides of the road, the time passing by and the direction he traveled.

Sure, I can pray he thought.

"Jesus, pray God forgives me when I get where I'm going."

Chapter 23

4/11 Windsor Bridge

In a magazine it was a fantasy. Look out there.

A photograph. There, look.

Somebody walks across a hammered parking lot. Another un-
laden flatbed noisily passes back behind on the right side. They
repainted the stripes after the ruts were made, crisscrossing the old
patterns so they don't try to go about with not a sound. A crackle
across the street from in the tire shop breaks through thick cold
grey fog.

Dean thought he might be able to get out of here.

A tractor waiting ahead begins the slow rumble. A noisy beast.

A page in today's history.

"Tell me what you saw."

It's not raining today.

More road?

"Was it close to freezing last night?"

"All the way to the next stop, no sweat."

He's good.

"About time to drive some more?"

Not ten minutes left.

Chapter 24

4/12 Pueblo, CO

So, they would ask if he had gotten tired.

"Hurry, you'll be late as usual."

"Okay, I'm almost ready, just give me another minute."

"Can't you just get up earlier?"

"I tried...next time?"

"No next time, you'll always be late, even to your own funeral."

"That's not true. I'm just running a little bit behind."

"A little behind, you missed the bus."

"I don't take the bus, you know that."

"Right, but if you did, you would never make it."

"Is there something wrong with my car?"

"Can't you see you can't keep thinking its okay to be late. You have to get there before eight. Its always five 'til when you leave."

"Okay but I'm never late."

"Someday you'll be late, and you won't have a job."

"I'm not late, you've be telling me the same thing from before we met, please stop."

"Don't get smart."

"Sorry, but..."

"So you get my point?"

"Yes, you're right and so is a loose couple of minutes playing a video game."

"Precisely, those electric things."

"Oh well, I'll limit my time, put them away for a while."

"Great, hey how is that electric car thing working out for you?"

"Super, clean and quiet too. Once I get past Fredrick, the magnetic flywheel smooths and can I get up around 200."

"Yes... I could see where going too fast from here to there could be dangerous. So maybe a minute to I-70 and then four to get to Cumberland."

"I'll ask them to schedule an earlier entrance window today, okay?"

Don't ask me to decide for you, you can do whatever it is you're doing. Anyway, since your not here, I am getting more time to finish another project. The over-land magno-tram from Bourney is about complete, we have both pedestrian sections working and well, don't ask any more about it, that's all I hear."

"I didn't start, you did."

"Yeah uh, guess we don't have a lot of time to talk anymore."

"Look I gotta go now, sorry."

Yeah, okay, okay...bye."

"Okay bye."

Yes, he recalled how wary and so tired. And long miles, and more no-sleep-nights were all that he remembered. Then, he'd drift into the conscious sleep and the thoughtless time, where his mind could rest.

Steve would ask if his ears were still ringing from the whine of the engine. His legs probably would have fallen off if he ever had walked as far as he'd driven that day. Too tired to walk. And of course, the weather got colder. Somewhere west out from Kentucky temperatures changed.

He thought about lighting a candle to try calming nerves.

“You were in my thought, and I prayed for you.”

Sometimes things just seem to move around. It was time again.

Chapter 25

4/14 Georgetown, CO

Blanco stopped in time once to catch a happy hour buffet at the local tavern. He was heading west, up into the mountains and away from Denver.

On the last night, as the darkness of the empty world circled around the black cab, he had to recall if where he'd stopped if anyone would be there in the morning. It never occurred whether something would happen before he fell off to sleep. Never heard any trucks pull-up that night, nor did he hear anyone leaving.

He rested.

With hot early sun roasting away a morning dew, a young cowboy poked his head in over the curtain.

"Time ya started up again", he yelled.

Blanco did not answer. Like an old diesel motor, silver smokestack pipes pushing up and puffing out thick grey smoke rings, people believed he would be around onto forever. He fell off asleep.

Chapter 26

4/24 St. George, UT

Sorrow songs of some past times and lost friend.

He fell silent, kept those feelings away.

Once Blanco said, "Has to be a school for happiness somewhere, the How to Be Happy Academy."

"I don't think money can buy it. And it's not just one certain thing or person, not a place to make you happy. Happiness is something that is everything and to be full of this emotion means a connection inside, that sends the spark of life beaming out so others can feel what you feel."

Pierce thought for a second, where he was, what he could do. Already seen plenty of hurt, not close to be able to share any happiness, too lonesome and isolated. Where he found life was when moving to the horizontal light, that that time moved the fastest. A portion of his lot slowed.

He sat motionless watching the twin sets of smoke-stacks move off even slower than when they appeared. More grave noises, quieting to dead silence again.

Chapter 27

Rain poured, waves streaming in with large pelts dropped down as he drove along a stretch of open highway, no lines on a road he couldn't see, he left desperate and crossed into gob-smacked. Watching a small pelt as it landed, all the splatters lined up to the splendid directives of discorded time.

Dean caught a picture of cool dampness as it was cold and the rains seeping of nature, the senses of soaking hair and his skin straight through. Some snowflakes caught the tops of the edges of windshield-wipers. Mother's wildness.

Resting in those daytime slumbers, he recalled the red rubber car on a beach some place down in to deep Panama. Along the mountain roads and down in a jungle of saturated greens and grey, an a old Opel wagon drifting along finding only eroded deserted waterbound cliffside. From nowhere then, they are by the ocean, its expanding wall blocking the horizon. They twist down closer and closer to another bunch of shacks made to look like a village near to shore, and the wheel moves pointing us at a sideways place to park. He pulls back the top flooding us with new sun.

"Play here, don't go swim," she says.

And its this time the little red toy tumbled out into clear water waves. Just as clearer thought that morning, it vanished. As if by chance or luck, maybe both, somebody big tried to catch what they thought was something floating, only to see the gurgle and laughter of another bubbly wave smacking back at them.

"It's nowhere, its lost."

"Yes, we can stop." Rain would wash away hurt for another yesterday, and move our ken to the next.

He could see tomorrow, a fresh start in life. Even trees seemed to smile, wet sloppy pelted leaves waiting to be part of any real life.

Chapter 28

5/4 Southern Alabama

Large wheels didn't take long to stop once they've been pulled off the rim. That black boat's long trailer slid along sideways soon after the brakes clamped down. Godfrey never realized at first how delayed he would be. Another car slid to his pathway, and unable to swerve from another one holding the lane, and he held on. Up ahead two people were working tediously on another car at the left side, and they hadn't been any luckier to find the rest of a tire lying in front them.

As its trailer began to drift onto the side lane, he lost more control with each instant. Unsure, he let off pulling and began pushing his big boat. Pushing toward the entertainment side of the roar. Still not certain, he watched as two figures ran back, waving as they jumped further to the muddier shoulder side. Both mirrors barely passed the other, and looking back to end of the trailer, the light swished them, only inches from their broken down truck.

And that's what happened,

Five hours later, back on the way, tracking and thinking. How deep into South Cal he could run?

Chapter 29

Buda, TX

To fast is not to eat.

Fasting wasn't systematic although he felt he had to fast as driving past. Fasting seemed right sometimes, to keep up. He couldn't explain any of it except to say he never recalled being slim again. Otherwise, dulled apparent apprehension was companion to first departures.

"Why then was an arm always first, then needed?"

What detail did that cure, not to say details always required attention. Now a different look at the same thing only over again.

This was it, the way he exposed and explained it since returning.

"The cowboy was a natural western quark," Pierce smiled back, "like back teeth falling out and answering back all at the same time."

OK, fasting to clear schemas, the memes. At first, as if an appropriate natural vector to a weaker self. But as the apparent malnutrition aspects of dieting become noticeable, his desperate searches lacked concentration, but the primal drives sharpened.

Pierce always seemed driven, and I had slowed down he'd say.

Sailing, we were sailing.

Chapter 30

Western Utah

What had been the point of the fight?

Fast.

And slow.

The quiet times in the hustle were okay for now, it was closer to Christmas.

Colder nights. The quiet world again.

Vachlor gambled around with the safety, on for a touch of restful sleep.

Pierce parked away time, back from rainy streets but not too far and slept.

"It's purposeful to look for the right stations and to find refuge." I'd heard him say once.

In time, books filled all empty space and in the time between he wrote her less, as if to know she would feel the frustration he felt, doomed at times and a finale as if necessary, so much unlike getting hair trimmed back from her collar or away from your eyes.

Time home passed more quickly.

He'd thought about the rope. Total Vachlor wonder.

He walked back from the lodge, past a white fence and noticed the small gate with some rope, knotted and holding a large white lock from closing. With the slightest cold wave, it would swing so many times that it'd marked an arch across the wood boards. The knot at the end, it also liked to have some meaning too, another time perhaps and an essence to everything. The sway of the pendulum to the other side.

Vachlor was working on a better slip knot still.

Chapter 31

East Palestine, OH

It started complicated. Missing Park Ave., pegging Taggart's empty lot to swing off.

A saga. Poetry. Adventure. A twist of time.

He had crossed early into Connecticut.

That night rain fell hard again. Lots of hills and a slow lengthened final drop.

Matt would sing along sometimes.

Try as he could, he'd always catch a radio wave and turn up the dial.

"I was spared at length,
when I was a young boy,
I looked and saw the concrete wall.

Now we look at the land.
An' what walls held back,
and measure our time."

Pierce would put in there, run into sleep.

Tomorrow, he'd stop early, and turn the boat around.

Still napped, only just to nap.

The ground held trains that night, about maybe nine or more. Some were very noisy. Some were very heavy. Others slipped up to and over midnight.

What sleep? He couldn't sleep, never much, but finally it stopped, and he drifted off. Sweetened sleep again.

Measurably large billets.

Chapter 32

Taos, NM

Any town, a pueblo then perhaps due for a stop that night. He' traveled the old routes between the big roads a lot. Into another month. Growing wary as the trips went on.

"Life is poor and those I love have left me," Pierce said, "so my body is sick and I cannot be part to any feast."

Faded paint, some shuttered broke window in a vacant building.

"I see no one who I once knew, my home is locked and quiet now, the old lantern lamp light flickers."

That tattered curtain has faded to yellow.

"I hear new snow falling too."

Railings always need repair. The traveler's miles last a might longer than time itself, as if it projects some type of heavier burden all forward to an endless path of jaded fear.

Again, a hill to slow you down.

"I grow older and sleep less, only to wake at night, and sit straight up in bed."

How can I stand to be lonesome. My body and soul yields to changes. So, it has been for years now. Countless nights. And all in quiet silence, I do not understand. Some old night and trying to stay warm.

Break of a day, a coffee inside a run-out hotel café, with a yellow floating blinker hotel "Single Rooms" sign rooms. Free muffins and warm hands.

Chapter 33

West Chicago, IL

A cowboy song coming in on the radio. Wheels dancing on a paved grey road. The wind only holding you back. Time on your side.

"In the night, a deer neatly crossed the road, in front he seen 'em, in frighten blank eyes, full soleum an it always sayin you saw it."

The north wind wrapped around the shell of the wagon, any hot engine slowly cooled everything down. Dalton passed through another day of logic-less frustration. All of his choices narrowed to a spirit dweller in the midsts, those muses.

"Weren't you here before. Did I see you?"

"Did you pick up the contact here before?"

"No, I just got here. I saw you fifteen minutes ago when I walked in."

"Then this is your first time here."

"Yes. It's my first time. I don't remember being here before. The noise is so loud."

Maybe another lifetime. Only you can recall it. As though you were there before.

Maybe then Pierce had been there.

He did not see the person again only until he showed himself. And he entered from the side. Maybe he was the one stuck in a middle, tasked to take people. They remembered his older face. But what happened?

He did not see him again.

Suppose he was waking.

Chapter 34

Savannah, GA

Sky rain again. Pierce walked for a while as the rain gathered in puddles and low ponds. A tireless, thankless job to fill gouges in the ground. Some days light peered out, and dawn cursed the western blackness. Blue colors of a clear spring. Walking in the blue drops brings him down to a clearing alongside a busy road. You're empty and waxed whole again, and you think about tomorrow. A thousand boys could never understand you. What loss was love you never could know. When do strangers return to places they've been.

Before then.

"Some kind of shun, distance."

"Pierce, what is it really? All that hatred out there."

"Uh, no..."

"You go ahead, did you look for me?"

"Look ahead, why look?"

A.M. silence, cars shake off the blowing winds. Why even try?

"I just can't pretend."

The rain is pounding on the roof. The winds rock me back and forth only to leave off again. A sudden wave breaks calm as sprinkles spatter my windshield.

"You can't go back. If you forgot something or it got thrown away, its lost."

Waiting for a way to get there, you give yourself a way.

How quickly forgotten, they compel everything.

"What's it like Pierce? You, who may know or, are you trying to recall any parts?"

That cast away, a finale, the long time gone, the changes.

Mother unwrapped the morning calm.

Raise the boat sail Rigger and run us the ken down away from this island sea, as these waves are still calm and slip beneath your cup. Right by mid-day, sail to our ship's shadow.

Chapter 35

Hinesburg, VT

At times he could sleep. And if a train passed along the slips of time, he could breathe deeply while everything rumbled past. And when sleep had not found Pierce, he was lost in the light of folded pages. She told him to write, he could not write. Faster, read, but it was to no end. And music would entertain him. We both had same favorites, about the Spanish of course. We wouldn't be back again.

"Why?" she asked.

Because we were alive then. It took a long time to explain, like angels on winds. Why did he write, did she tell it to you? Could he try say to see it rightly to say and to jot it down?

He guessed she knew a lot more about it, she wasn't only a dream.

Chapter 36

Where do you write a story of the last legendary refugee of the American Spirit of freedom? The start out west, where still deep blue evening skies have eagles aloft, along some instantly quiet outback town, when our youngest dreams of screaming cruisers blazing across the night were heard?

From distances far away, he hears nations abound out on stretches of roads. On our distant pathways, each finds their way.

He'd sit hours listening to an old FM radio. Sometimes he'd sit buckled to the wing seat just to stare out, waiting for any rumble from the weight of heavy machines breaking down some big earth chunks.

Chapter 37

Hurricane, UT

Sometimes he'd wait. Unwitting flightless journey. Never found much to do when he would wait. He seemed finally resolved to move from the unwelcome straight dead boredom to direct primal submission.

Para-phrasing that famous phrase from Joan Didion, he "stood in the sun on the Western street waiting for the young agent down from the Utah office to back her Corvette past the Federal building to where he was.

First a flurry of activity to begin, to start out again.

Beyond ennui, more than from boredom than irritation of a somewhat specific sort of boredom, the view of weary sanctity given an obdurate existence of living a life with too much ease, and at which he visits with its "pale unrest" such like an anti-proton.

Asking him, he could read more into these classics, he'd belong as any tribute to any modern morality, less any staggering twitch of those electrical synapses.

Some restless sleep.

Awakened.

Drove.

Fuel.

Rain stops, rest area.

Slept

"Saw chickens on the shoulder side, the big road again. They were all dead. Surely never believed once they ever even belonged there."

"He'd guess they jumped."

Thought maybe they fell off.

Perhaps they tried to fly out, tried to get off that old chicken truck. Could a wind or something sometimes blown them out from them cages? Many bumpy roads from in Mexico perhaps, it pitched them?

How could ever but so evenly they all drop down off, take a ride off a stretch of heaven's country highway?

Chapter 38

Terrebonne, OR

The midnight rocks… in the imaginations.

There is no hesitation. Pull the anchors up and turn this boat astern, as if voices on any winds calls.

Not a thing more to say, he stays throwing it all away.

"We would not be back, won't be back again." Pierce never thought he would come to find he'd be gone before the day returned.

In Merlin's time, he remembered her as an awakening day, not for long in passing, the lost kingdom aglow in time's wrinkles. Down through ages of blue invaders from across a froze North Ocean, how time bent you to expect your years. Lost memories well faded and from them an ancient magic still lingers.

When the passage ahead narrows and a slight of broad sword from my black saber, he would not change my mind. A brightly beamed reflection as this spark dowsed that gladiator's red pain, and his anger summoned.

A red dragon to slay.

Chapter 39

Our sun faded.

He had to get away, to leave.

Just attack, you seem bound to fall.

I'm broken, see what is you in a safe zone?

Do you need to turn?

Chapter 40

… to find an end.

Why do we stay on? From the beginning, he could live his lives over and over again.

And in the blink of an eye.

No shadows in the winds while he waits.

"Pierce look out again and then the change."

Chapter 41

Prairie City, OR

Never be un-amazed from your companion, their imagination is quite an industrious mind. Always imagining something different, and something better. And a cost at always more than enough. Machines counted the how many times he did everything to traverse thin expanses, his conclusive types of time locked analysis.

"Would park almost, he could get this trailer in from off the pavement anywhere."

Cold rocks? Then, and again the same thing over again. The people and their things he hadn't seen before, it's all here and so noisy.

Some places where its quiet and he hears splashing waves and gulls dodging in-between each other, morning sand-castles crumbling from salty waves.

The slow walk along the beach to feel the sun and sand, maybe.

Chapter 42

Reno, NV

Ever experience some wall in some jungle and were skeptic at the instant some part of it wasn't real, and then come back? That happened.

He climbed it and looked over. The gross plains and those mountains as solid imagination grew.

Pierce thought he could just leave, set sail. Rig another day, find his tall ship pulling away at some sunken anchor, pulling and casting a frost up and he would forget her. True almost while reaching out and stirring in his sleep. The tingly feeling of warm sun gave to thawing in his frozen cheeks and nose. Come mid-morning and a bitter snapping from outside, noises from camp ramps up. Folding lawn furniture, the broken that one didn't make the cut. He tried to pretend he wasn't ill.

Mac sat uncomfortably across from Pierce in the westernized diner booth. Leaning over into the corner, he watched him scratch at his arm where a tattoo of an American flag had faded and then with the other reach inside his shirt pocket for a wad of bills. Across sat a very fat person cloaked beneath a soiled old brown cap that barely covered the back of his fat head. His hat kept the remains of matted messy black and greying hairs sticking out in all directions. His dark eyes plopped behind his sizable nose, and his whiskers and the uneven sideburns were bunched up in bushy mixes of strands against his ears. He sat noisily with his panso pushed up against the table and shirt sleeves rolled up, and both his hands clung underneath thick crossed arms covering most of the top of his well rounded pot-belly. Well, when he lit another cigarette,the big pink skinned nose twisted into a red balloon.

Dodging the first puff of nasty smoke as it drifted up past him back in his hide-out, he felt Mac push the table with his fat belly.

"I'm frozen in here!" He cried another churning cloud of smoke curling up his mouth and floating toward Pierce.

He looked back at Mac's face and at the fat red knob.

"Weather turned bad on us again."

As they finished and Mac got up to leave, he looked back and shook his finger.

"Wasn't sure last pickup. Last night I checked."

"Then I'll call," said Pierce.

Chapter 43

Gallop, NM

You are everywhere.

I am not alone.

"The people had many types of council from time to time."

Errand man went all round to call the people to these councils.

At one council Coyote arose and said: "First, we must change our rule about death, because all are not being treated alike. Now when some die, they come back to their people, and then others die and never see their people again. I propose to make another rule, so that we may all be treated alike after death."

Silence in the hushed tent, the council of elders whispering lifted the tribe.

"This is the rule purpose, when anyone dies, let him be dead forever and let no living person ever see him again. Our Great Father above made a place every one of us may go after death."

"Now when anyone,'" Coyote said, choking back from the rising smoke, "passes, he shall go from the living forever, but we shall still keep up the fires for six days."

All the people nodded for Coyote's speaking, and so, from that time on, even to present day, same rule is kept. When anybody dies, he is gone forever.

"Never to return again," said Coyote, "our people are taken to the sky when they die and become the stars we see at night."

Pierce heard this old Indian story told and descry some wolves may have eaten the tribes dried meats.

Feed the good wolf.

Chapter 44

Tulsa, OK

At that convergence point, Chase's search for time to shape a life's zephyr. What decided how it is, what he could do? Clearly of the people holding him, they were looking back but don't look and see them looking. How many people has he seen now on that road.

Like priests?

Everyone remembers. And I looked at him.

Had they already seen him?

It's past. Whether they did or not, intentionally or as fate would have you, it is the midst of change, it was all conveyed.

So, a resurfaced memory.

"Who was Chase?"

Chapter 45

Nevada

The dark saber moved along at gladiator speed, boiling past the horde of some other beaten time grown dithery fighters. Cool crisp rains came to the higher deserts sooner as expected. A cold thick coat frosted tiny tin buildings and cars. There were no birds.

He wouldn't sleep as what he'd felt as fear chased his thoughts. The vocation chosen, the submission into unwarranted freedoms. More of deliverance back away from times of tidy aprons and of faith worshiping at that grocery store, and chosen for misty mountain mornings, Indian beads, and eagle's feathers. His choosing to move away from any convention, straight to the frying pan of all collective fears echoed, he'd only a glimpse of the endless quarks of time.

Another time of waiting.

In balance to any experience between good and bad, the dominant conventions move along truth bound. For the ordinary, those taking the factor of something supernatural into consideration, Pierce's liken phenomenon of the runner persona with its thick shielding blanket propped against the dark layers of daily life.

He thought to drive more. Further?

"Yes certain-," the voice stopped. No wait. Find some strength to keep moving. Undoubtedly, his end of the rope was edging closer, a fringe existence no longer welcoming to his human soul. Then yes, hearts wept.

The long way home.

"How long since the last time my eyes rested at home?"

To the end, all the way home again.

Quit!

"Tell the wind not to blow."

A push up the next hill would help.

Chapter 46

Helena, MT

The food, the line, it seemed okay. So he couldn't but fly past to find a table two chairs. Some kind of a local place, full of four-seat booths and only the corner space seemed nice. An older color TV on the wall with CNN weather. The windows tinted silvery, darkened out but lots of life from inside, but not much.

The menu is old, and the plastic cover looks a tatter-yellow. The first picture he sees, a short stack plus a well-cooked sausage patty, or two. You think maybe eggs and some toast but no, it's the effect. Plus, the altitude of fluffy pancakes. A regular syrup, some strawberry and maple and blueberry.

Any thoughts of hunger and the road are shaken as his light-headed attention gets drawn to a waitress standing in the pattern in the pictures on the menu.

"Coffee?" she asks.

Chapter 47

Arlington, Va

The meeting at the diner in VA was only a beginning to twelve different and deadly commissions over a course of seven years. Tracer money was watched as well as any odd or seemingly 'out-of-place' persons were tagged and followed up on. Travel shutdowns in early 2020 and airlines quit posting scheduled forecasts of incoming, their foresight provided us notice to expect surges in counter-intelligence and hacking. We followed one lead into southern Louisiana bayou country. Clearly lost us in the swamp.

In the fall, the skin on the back of his hands tightened even more with the changes to cold. The smooth muscles cooled more quickly, and our muffled conversations were kept low. We'd moved to where they pointed and came around to park at the North side of the Capital. Security checked us in, and we were escorted to a new "pitch-hit" zone.

Pierce was moved to the single door exits soon after the shutdowns started.

"LT, we're on station."

"Copy."

My piece was holstered, safety lock visibly on. We waited only a few short minutes hands on earpiece, stood anticipating an exit door to be opened. Following seven short months working national tensions and deadly encounters with extremists, our detachment battery was downsized even more so we wore encrypted comm with upgrade hardware but still we were stretched.

Never.

That morning, the people's business started up as usual. Station and wait, those two directives were agency triggers.

Chapter 48

Pierce lost contact to many of the people he encountered. Missions never ceased, and he held to his vision. Somethings moved on long narrow lines, and he aged endlessly.

"Our shoes became worn and tore as we moved down and grew older."

"Matt still attracted a pretty smile and mysterious eyes."

An easy life became troublesome. Sometimes he fell away from doing most physical labor. Home was no longer the goal. Raining more, he walked a while thinking what must fill the eternity of time when they'd laid to rest another hero. The daytime darkness boiling away, sun rays peering down. Racing through in the vast keep of the blue sky. His breath sent him into a clearing alongside an empty road, whole again.

"He never really knew sometimes why he'd ever made it back."

Understandably, not knowing didn't bother him as much as finding out sometimes, he was no longer searching to go. He just couldn't continue at the pace he was driven much longer.

"It didn't matter."

Time was walled up hard and even so, it ticked away again later at some micro-mini distant instant.

Chapter 49

7/30

To Dalton,

I would like to trade some collector cards.

"When I was an adolescent, we collected things."

Oh?

Well do you want to trade any cards with me?

Pierce asked him, "Yes, or no?"

Care to trade some collector cards.

Don't you, have some? To trade?

"I've to go ahead now and lock the trailer door."

Chapter 50

Montana

Quit looking at the begging man, he's been seen looking back at you for all of some instant. It wasn't wrong and not for him to judge your person. That's where he is and where he has been. Now he moves on, begging still.

"I figure I be on my way, too."

On down the road to the next hill. Lost in America on the way.

Chapter 51

Western Montana, ~ 4/27

Look, you don't want to see what I saw today.

"Well, it wasn't pretty."

"I saw life on the road. Some cars flipped over; a trailer pushed off into woods."

"A dump truck rolled over."

"Dead animals."

"An ambulance."

"Two smoky-bears at the weigh station, some trailers left at stops."

"Cattle." He spoke.

Pierce glanced over at Dalton, "a farmer riding along on an old-time silver tractor throwing thick smelly brownish-black fertilizer out."

"Lots of hills, and purple sages."

"White bluffs."

And once again, a silver-orange disc came up while moon faded away in its fullest quarter, a wide and broad horizon opened across from the fields. Wind, sun and water, and the moon pushes and pulls beasts around. By the still of morning she dusts him down.

Chapter 52

Two lanes

He kept going. He couldn't stop, not even if he wanted to.

The eyes in the back of his head shifted rapidly, he caught Pierce glance away to fall asleep. He could not sleep now. Speeding through time, a hands weight to control the shutter, it goes on and he cannot stop. Just as soon as he'd caught himself, his eyes searching out, the road-way kept going further. Feeling and watching subtle brown bumps on the road through the wheel. He's awakened again to such uneasiness of sitting up, and the feeling of swaying, buffeted again from shifting off the ruts of the road. The quick glance through a rear-view mirror to see.

"Did anyone run off the lane?" He asks himself.

"No, thank the good Lord Jesus, no one back there." Pierce's open mouth and wide eyes were reactions to patterns.

"Really need to pay more attention," he said, watching the trailer out the passenger side, "and look back."

Looking out from under the window's visor to north, stars stilled to all line up again, all brights. Timeless links to lives from beyond all this. Never a last moment, never a final goodbye. These are always there, never waiting to be.

He moved through time.

Chapter 53

His sunny day faded in the western edges of sky, the AI feed kept a thread of steady ads for mold, rodent infestations, and suicide help. The year 2355 was a hundred years after a Kremlin had dropped a bomb. Nearly overnight the real world ceased. Pierce knew from the small tribes living around fringe bombed out areas about resistance and survival, it seemed bound in obtunded reflexes.

Kretl met him at the portal only minutes after they arrived.

Drifting down to a steady slow speed he looked out.

From beneath an issue micro-protonic switching transit suit and plabicent-bicon helmet, he could feel and see some of the silver-blue blur. A great tension releasing task. Justice walking along, loaded pieces, they'd all dropped into the silvery white-stained dust of region W3K88.

Experience intense. Some things couldn't crystallize in the smaller matter-analysis discs.

"What day is it?"

"Thursday, but that's not even certain."

They'd jumped center into a large warehouse structure in the industrial zoned estate housing with some small camps and set out armored batteries in circular bunkers covering the higher open range. In the heart of the village were parallel two story blocks set back against the low level brick building, which was fronted by all types of vehicles, painted, armed and bound to ruin enemy workshops. Slippery silver sand-bagged crossing points. The technic music could be heard with the "thump-ting" of the mechanic work sounds.

He'd been taken down, field worked over 40 years, and not seen much reason to tolerate anything anymore from anybody. Pierce had been seemingly leaning toward and taken a draw to move into time collections. Arriving with him were thirty-nine trained jump-team members. They'd all had billets with no meanings or futures, and so each one signed. A ferocious battle inevitably ensued, and jurisdictions made sure sometimes those excursions neither happened or anyone knew about it. No one ever could find out why the Big K moved. Reactionary or fate, our news followed all the comm threads and then finally we would read we were being replaced.

Sure, some time-tunnel misunderstandings were about due, but not forever.

Two twin-sized forest green SUV sleds waited. Pierce looked up over the track tires and kick panels. A grey tube extended thru the pulsing green globe and snaked down under the passenger area. A pulsing glow of reverse gray glowed purple. Shielded door covers and frack-pads strapped to loaded mine-pod containers buckled by 2.4TI Magno-trigger mechanisms, the metal lined grey cable ran down into the front grill on both sides from behind the single phased modified laser cannon. Simple, effective radically controlled energy, and a steering wheels.

"Where are we going off today?"

Pierce knew, they'd be sent into areas in a zone transferring into future time. Walled up and shimmering, touching with nothingness and the forces bent around reality, it was Duncan who first explained it to him.

As the group filtered out one-by-one, no one ever looked back once. A woman was waiting on a two seater type of floating surfer bike, complete with sails and an anchor. A55 unabashedly wrapped his knapsack around the sissy-bar, kissed her and jumped on. He was more truly a real manly man, but his excited ignorance exhaled danger, and we knew eventually McDermitt would need help from getting in trouble.

Everyone had their ways to finding home.

Next to a small building sided up to a broken-down wall, a bluish-grey wolf stood looking. He was seeing us as food, not looking for friends. At his back were two more his size, as he was more toward five feet at the shoulders, so its teeth and head were level to the top of the SUV. Could it maybe have been a bad omen? Anyway we certainly moved a bit quicker and loaded up.

Our transport slipped off quickly, mostly snapping us back as we shot away.

"I can't breathe, and I need a helmet," someone in the rear said.

"Helmets on, buckle-up, we're going to yellow, indications are not ignored, we're in contested areas. Stay low, were moving."

"Pierce, it's not me." He pointed at the reflections in the stars.

"A bit of it works and the rest of it doesn't matter much."

Chapter 54

Cruz pulled the carrier to a stop between an alley and the street, turned about and eased forward, as to look for someone following close behind us. The carrier's grey outside and neatly arranged armor-bars were possibly to hide it in yellowed streetlights and the two large black-strap bags across the travel rails helped blend us in with the dark alleyway. The boot was laden with fiber boxes and extra ops equipment converted to back-ups, plus room for two agents. An electric step connector made for solid footholds along the carriage which anchored welded on long hardened steel rods beneath.

He turned us into the alley with the sloshing grace of a blundering lost fat man, the lights dimmed ahead as he eased us forward.

"See anything?"

Pierce turned looking up and motioned. "No, let's keep moving."

Armed and strapped in for a country road race, both four-man teams turned and moved to the center building, gloves and power-lasers hoisted and red. Now, not far behind and advancing, another follow-up team blocked the entrance. A two-person detachment suited up for field work pushed up front and stopped, only shy to where they quickly vanish. We all at once loaded up more gear.

Protected and served.

Was the duty worth any more than experience?

"Hey Pierce, wake up! Over there, next to the walk, up. Someone's there." Blanco said. The silvery light behind someone in a pitch-dark alcove appeared.

"Hold."

"Where is he at?" Fletcher asked.

"Matt, drop forward follow us. We are walking in right now."

A door opened, and he slid out. We listened to the safety click as he walked along.

"There."

Up front, Pierce forced up a loose article bag and jammed it against the front window. The door handle clicked, and he aimed.

Humming engines was all they could hear.

Chapter 55

When both rear doors dropped and the shell top slid off, Matt pulled back to clip down the 50 cal.

"Bamm, bamm, ca'chinke, ca-chink"

He dove to the wheel as they rattled down. Over his right shoulder another two debts jumped and dove up over the wall, and ducked behind him, struggling to lean back without falling.

"Bam...bamm, bamm sss, bamm...sssss."

Cruz picked up.

We watched as the front end tipped up and the rear wheels cleared the median. It bounced hard against the slick asphalt, jumped both lanes and crashed into an embankment, pinning the two in their BMWe.

Pierce looked annoyed and imperceptible so we couldn't hear a thing but knew what he was saying.

Chapter 56

He'd found himself awol for weeks and at home in hopes of a time to retire, when but someways the eye of the FBI could be seen in the woods.

And as fate would weigh in, on a quick errand he was moving and warming the big block up with quick full fast acceleration landing area, managing to run quicker and through all eight pulls within yards. What wasn't in line of sight at zero, and just before letting up, there he was.

No doubt, lights on and a big "honnnkk" to tie up at the pier.

"Open your window."

He rolled the window down, looking back at the outlines of perhaps the biggest and baddest greyed-out silver black SUV he'd ever seen before.

"Am I free to go?"

License and registration.

Did I do something wrong?

Went through the stop light back there, did you see it?

Oh man, he thought, "Oh yes, I missed that one."

"Any reason why"

"No. I didn't see traffic and its late." Thinking about remembering it flashing. But the car lights were flashing, right in his rearview mirror. Sort of out of focus but seriously flashing, and with no particular sequence. If without question it was an alien space UFO then he would never know.

"Where were you coming from?"

"Oh, just some business. Live just right up past the airstrip."

"Okay, wait here."

Without a doubt he knew getting a ticket may be in his directed near future. He didn't want to meet any new friends and was already tired from a long drawn-out day packed with meetings. An inspector phoned for the certification for hot armor storage at the new armory, so everything was safe. The big 5.0 swelled just under 1K as it rumbled down to a purr.

"Okay sir, like your sticker."

Oh, the fed, yeah got that over in Virginia."

So, I 'm giving you a warning, a lot of accidents at that intersection, so slow down."

Pierce knew he'd not only dodged a huge bullet, but also skated back home without having to say anything.

Chapter 57

We were weighed.

He chased the sun until it fell back beyond another horizon. All day long it seemed he couldn't keep up under that grey dotted sky, he ducked into an endless pillow of clouds. It rained part of the way.

Look out. See there.

She must've spun out in the rain, landed back in that ditch. She's under an umbrella with a cell phone stuck to the side of her head now, and frantic. But why not? Because it all happened with a short squeeze if a sequence of time.

At one instance everything seemed okay, then Mother had her way.

Pierce longed for the sun as it fell behind the mountain.

It seemed like an early morning, a damp thick fog to depend on. Cool rain cleaned the air. The air only smelled good again.

Chapter 58

Italian Summer '57

A hot Italian summer heat had gotten Tru. Bugs from the tall grass nipped his arms and legs. He had been given a pair of shorts and a T-shirt to wear and shed the cloth tennis shoes so he could feel the warm beach sand between his toes. Excitement from the little campground in Tuscany buzzed as he and six other children from other families played and laughed while parents sat around an old wood table talking and smoking cigarettes. A bottle of red wine thump and the FM radio sounds meshed the clink-clink of wine cups as it teetered on a camp shelf, the radio announcer saying "take the tour, take the tour."

Tru's father found a very good place to park the car and trailer, and he'd opened the pop-up to four beds and a mini dinette. He also unloaded the sleeping bags and other suitcases from the trunk. Tru's mom was immediately busy rattling plastic forks and separating paper plates to put lunch out of fresh bread, cut meats & cheese, and red sodas. He took a quick look at his Timex watch and thought it said about two or so, which he felt was fine because it meant he had time to play for another six or seven hours before he was to be told to go to get ready for bed, again. The other kid's moms and dads were putting up their campers and spreading out sleeping bags as they also unpacked toothbrushes and towels and called for them to wash up for dinner and change clothes.

Tru caught the glimpse of some girl as he waved and slipped away into the pop-up. She had the talked a lot, and her eyes seemed to twinkle in the later afternoon sunlight.

"Come on everyone, let's eat," his Auntie Audre called as she stepped back out of the small trailer, "we're going see a leaning tower tomorrow."

"Ah, Mom don't want to, when are we going home." Elaine sang in her usual whinny voice while reaching for a paper cup and climbing into the picnic table. He thought to himself that she was almost eleven and had clearly been becoming the real pain for him during this vacation.

"You're going to have to change that, young lady," Audre said, "your father doesn't want this time spoiled by someone not enjoying themselves. Why not have a good time while we're here?"

"Auntie, are you going to shop around, find more food for to-morrow for these little kids?" Frank asked Sheila, her mom just as he popped his head out from around the back of the camper.

Tru remembered how happy and excited his father seemed when she decided to go along with us, that's what his mom had told Ellie.

"So, Auntie, where is the leaning tower?"

After a short dinner and more grown-up talk, he and the six other kids slipped away and concentrated on catching lighting bugs and throwing pebbles out to the water. Tru laughed and played until it was almost too dark to see them. He got tired then, and leaned next to his Pop from exhaustion while everybody sat around singing campfire songs and saying jokes and stories about factory work back home. It had taken them a day and a half to get to Italy, plus two years saving every brown penny he could find.

Chapter 59

The early morning sun began heating everything up immediately as Tru turned over to hide from daylight. Slipping on wet tennis shoes and shorts, Tru jumped up off to one side so he could see his father hooking up the chain to the car and swearing about something to his mother about folding chairs and clothes.

"Please get your toothbrush and take one of these towels. Go ahead with her, I'll be along in only a minute."

The two hurried along up the sandy pathway to an open shower bungalow. Turning to look, he could see the rich blue Mediterranean and the white seagulls swooping in for another bit of sand. A salty spray covered over the grassy areas where the crabs hide and the morning air caught him as he hopped along with his older sister and wondered what on earth was the tower of pizza, and if he could climb up it. Another seagull swooped to catch a lift off a strong breeze.

"Let go of my hand!" he screamed. "I know what I'm doing."

He stepped into the other shower side, the thick steamy mist blurring his eyes, the thick fog making him guess where the shower was. A long wooden bench bumped his leg as he could hear the noises from the steam call out for him to hurry, to get in the shower. He stripped and tiptoed in to see two other kids run past and sliding across the soapy tile floor. He could almost hear his sister on the other side saying something about some guy and his mom saying something back. As quick as he could pull on his sandals and slung his towel over his neck and shoulder, he bolted out the door swinging it open as a man with flip-flops and black sunglasses walked in past the sink.

Tru was worrying. They weren't in the woman's shower. He wondered if he should open the door and peek in, to check and see if they were there. A second thought he turned and started to run. He ran as fast and hard as he ever had to the spot where the car and camper parked. As he got to the top of the small mound between the tiny office and the seashore, he looked and saw all cars were gone and the campsites were empty.

By then, the watch said three and he was hungry waiting. A man with rubber flip-flops and red shorts had been fishing around all afternoon and caught some small fish. Now as the sun warmed up white sands, he watched that man wade out until almost waist deep in waves casting his line out further and deeper into the blue. It didn't make much difference to him until he saw the man's fishing pole almost bend in half. He watched. The man pulled and pulled the long fishing pole. Now almost neck deep in water, the fisherman finally pulled in a fish that looked about ten feet long to him from there, and he laughed as the man held the fish up out of the water and try to stuff it into a mesh bag.

"What has happened," he asked himself, "where has everyone gone? What was he going to do?"

"I don't believe they would leave without me," he thought to himself, "they couldn't just leave, maybe they forgot about me. I didn't do anything wrong, and Dad said we could go to the top of the tower. They'll be back.

Chapter 60

Before all it was nothing. No roads, no stops.

No stop-lights, no RR tracks. There was nothing out there. People like him carved out hollow shells of life to give back to their families the life they gave them. Life for life.

Does it matter, the ways their life is lived? In all sighted aspects of American history, freedom was the most powerful effect people needed and sought. As he considered their lives, Pierce thought how those ancestors survived.

"Pierce, wake up."

He didn't seem shocked by instinct. They had to have come from a radio signal. He watched to the side and out front again, speeding down through time. What radio? There was nothing where ever any radio could be. More frost, cold. He'd parked with less snow in Missouri. Seemed colder, not harsh dry. Colorado was dry. Tall misty drought country near a mile up. Shadow winds. Here, time sensitive stringy toppings, wait and he listens keyed in to survival with an empty wagon. Nothing from nothing, beyond your reach. You can't describe the stop at Commerce because it's all about the cowboys.

He sat there. Three hours he sat for two movies. Tired or without need, his time had run out.

Three cowboys, because that is the way they appeared. Pierce moved slowly along the counter toward the door not even noticing if they'd noticed his slight moves. The oldest one with blondish blackened hair, he struck first, a wilder side showing up. He'd watched them. Around the line of different color cars and trucks and across the asphalted part of the dirt lot. They appeared to follow one another although not immediate, seemingly without intent nor any concern, a western mosey along, mingling about with some of those waitresses smoking, the one straggler's booted run out across the paved section by the building neared being comical. But he looked stronger and with a certain forward headed take advantage-of-it-all gaze, and a full row of sparkly white teeth. That one quickly caught up to him and tightened the headlock-hold.

"Hey, you go see where he's headed," he'd heard the other straggler say.

The one with new blue jeans tightened up to the middle of his waist with a big buckle, and the other one, who's shirt sleeves were cut off and no longer attached anymore to cover his skinny white arms, they both ran across to a pickup truck down at the end of the row. A coffee can sized belt buckle balanced his gait as he took off, his bow-legged hurry-up run along had him bounding straight up and down with a kick of a stallion rider, and he seemed to show off as his boots scraped and slid by, trails of fine brown circling his clunky-clunk steps.

Then, all of the sudden that miniature Cowboy Bull-Riding with its rear legs kicked up and out belt buckle caught the sun and sparkled.

Chapter 61

His left eye opened slowly to the bright light from outside, the feeling was cold.

"It got strange to return. Even to places he'd been before."

The radio was still on.

He could hear two voices, one older man "some kind of paradise. All I want is what's real."

The other, "… all this hate?"

"No war."

"He'll go ahead."

"You go ahead."

AM. Silence. The cab shook off winter bursts of frozen choppy wind. Nathan tried opening the door as snowy drifts battered the door.

He heard the whisper, "not to pretend, the end changed."

Sitting and waiting and watching for another cool calm blue wave to float past along the wall in the jungle.

Chapter 62

The Blue Truck.

We began packing and loading.

The loading? Well, at first it stopped for eight years, then for another five quick months went as the muddled soft button off-ness ones were left to settle things out. Pierce never heard Angel complain. He needed the work, his wife taking on boarders as the movements started. In small towns most roads kept clear and clean it was just us out, close to narrow, yet opened up from work again different. Kept us from being in the wrong place every time.

Dust? Seemed dust never bothered us, we kept our noses covered and the warm tunnels kept the smell outside, not run in. As the evening sun would burn off the last bit of crusty earth, wiping off sweat, their thirsts were quenched. The other kids stood side by side and watched. Its big loud engine motor moving the big ship. Back to our backs we stood watch, some younger person would sing words out loud and we'd catch just his sayings, the moving words.

Back in the front of the trailer hooked to the blue truck we stacked in the heavier items and nudged boxes firmly together, and packing covers got thrown around bed posts and the dining room table, and pillow light boxes stuck to the walls. A section of locker boxes, buckled down in ranges of one ton found a way onboard. The items yellow "X" tagged and its number jotted down. Then more and more boxes until he thought the counting was over and perhaps maybe the last boxes loaded were from his room, and he watched closely at the man rolling the last few items in, brooding as the bike he'd bought with tip money was strapped onto the last saddle space.

So, sometime again later the blue truck stood up and rumbled, all packed and bulging, sleepy looking. The stray cat after catching a bird and eating it, stretching to its sides. A mouser game, meek as it watches mice search for water, they return. The dripping water-tap washing pains away . No shock and a long slender full bodied under-belly. It happened before and before again, and again before then.

And yet to be weighed.

Pierce wasn't sure the first time his path was deterred if he changed. He wasn't held. Travel became an angry expression to be overlooked, and the faster they fled and the darker it was, the easier it became to run.

When winter came we all slept. Awoken in the following mornings as the light returned, as the soft growing green peaks broke the ground, and mother held us. We were always here.

The older man said something to get everyone's eye and waved as large black puffed billows left the silver pipes. Another roar to the motor and the hiss of a snake. We jumped back as the blue truck pushed up and its rear wheels squatted down, nudging the load to move.

A long sword challenge fought across the Mesa top, the steps up his. Pierce dropped down into a deep crystalized pocket beneath the Mesa.

Chapter 63

Olive Tree

About noon-time we heard the noises and immediately ac-knowledged the ratcheting mechanic sounds. We geo-located them and started out running toward it, our eyes peeled back wide as our group flew off. Across the cool green mowed area and up past the sandy playground with the metal pipe swing set, we stopped just short of a big brown truck with a big metal crane. Three men were standing around it, while another one could be seen picking at the tree roots with his shovel.

The smallest of us kid stood jittering and asked, "… what's that?"

Back at the base, Col. Devlin glanced down at the order.

"What's done we do not forget."

Blanco stood up.

Nathan cursed under his breath.

Mitchel smiled a bit and said some little prayer, murmuring it to the two runners to his back, standing closest to the exit flaps of the tent. Leaning over to hear the Colonel's words, he bumped the old Recon-Tech up to the front of all the men.

"So, another one. Another we don't need or like no more. He's the thorn on this rose now."

"Well, he's gone, but the thought was from what will stay. The thought."

Pierce looked over to the others standing along the sides of the tent, and the empty place the General had often stood, as if hope would make him appear. Some positions changed.

"We lived with them, we stood with them, together and for generations. We are their decline. We are diminished surely, and now?" He looked over at two young officers, then over to the young group of Air Corp men, the enlisted ones.

Pulling back at the tent flap and glancing out, he turned inside to face everyone again.

"Look, what is left from this is not to be mourned over or fought about. What remains is still, and alive in the eternal time. The old expression "Here today, gone tomorrow." How excitingly true and fatally direct. Decedent and transcendent. From beneath and up above. They are the kings, the generals in our lives, and leaders... no less than famous."

He looked at the wood mail basket on top of the two plank boards set up as a desk and reached over at the orders on top.

"Well." he said looking over the groups of women and men gathered inside the tent. "As the long foreknown standing command Order 667, what you heard in the distance was noise of the old oak tree in housing. The General commended cutting it down days before he left us. We're only following orders."

THE END

Simon Rodriguez

Crystal City, Texas, 1957

"Greater hunters lived by meager means"

www.ingramcontent.com/pod-product-compliance
Lightning Source LLC
Chambersburg PA
CBHW070502300726

48975CB00007B/2290